Forward March!

Joan and the army rode into Orléans for their final battle. The men had been fighting for a long time. They had fought bravely, but their hearts and souls were weary. Joan did her best to rally her men for this final attack.

She commanded the trumpets to sound the attack. Wielding her sword, she cried out, "If there are a dozen of you that are not cowards, it is enough! Follow me!" Joan rode off and her men followed, inspired as they looked toward their young leader.

READ ALL THE BOOKS
IN THE WISHBONE *classics* SERIES:

Don Quixote

The Odyssey

Romeo and Juliet

Joan of Arc

*Oliver Twist**

*The Adventures of Robin Hood**

*Frankenstein**

*The Strange Case of
Dr. Jekyll and Mr. Hyde**

**coming soon*

Wishbone™ classics

Joan of Arc

by Mark Twain

retold by Patrice Selene

Interior illustrations by Ed Parker

Wishbone illustrations by
Kathryn Yingling

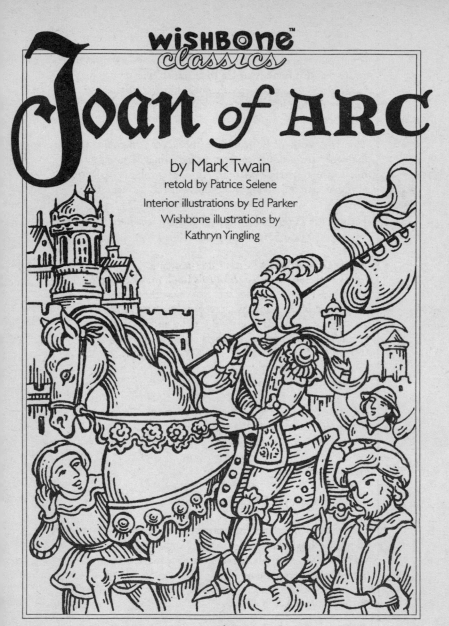

HarperPaperbacks

A Division of HarperCollinsPublishers

This is a work of fiction. The characters, incidents, and
dialogues are products of the author's imagination and are
not to be construed as real. Any resemblance to actual
events or persons, living or dead, is entirely coincidental.

HarperPaperbacks *A Division of* HarperCollins*Publishers*
10 East 53rd Street, New York, N.Y. 10022

Cover photographs by Carol Kaelson

A Creative Media Applications Production
Art Direction by Fabia Wargin Design
Edited by Matt Levine

First printing: June 1996

Printed in the United States of America

❖ 10 9 8 7 6 5 4 3 2 1

LOUIS DE CONTE

Introduction

All set to enter a world of action, adventure, drama, and laughs? Then come along with me, **Wishbone**. You may have seen me on my TV show. Often I am the main character and sometimes I am the sidekick, but I'm always right in the middle of a thrilling story. Now, I'm going to be your guide as we explore one of the world's greatest books — JOAN OF ARC. Together we'll meet a lot of interesting characters and discover places we've never been! I guarantee lots of surprises too! So find a nice comfy chair, and get ready to read with **Wishbone**.

Table of Contents

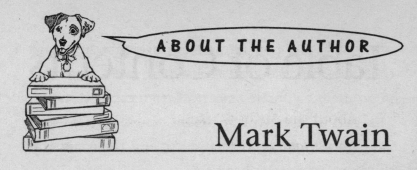

Mark Twain

I want to introduce you to one of the greatest American writers, Samuel Langhorne Clemens. You've never heard of him? Well, you might know him by his pen name: Mark Twain.

Often a writer uses a pen name to hide his or her identity, but Mark Twain also used his pen name to pay tribute to the Mississippi River. Twain spent his childhood on the banks of the Mississippi, and the river was the setting for some of his most exciting adventure stories!

Samuel Clemens was born in 1835 and grew up in Hannibal, Missouri, a town on the Mississippi River. Young Samuel loved life on the river, and as a boy he dreamed of becoming a Mississippi riverboat pilot. When he became a writer, Samuel Clemens selected as his pen name a phrase that he heard echoing across the great river—*mark twain*. Riverboat pilots used the phrase *mark twain* to measure distance. The call of *mark twain* meant the river was two fathoms (about twelve feet) deep, and the water was therefore safe for the riverboat.

Mark Twain's father died when he was twelve, and at that time he had to quit school and go to work as a printer. While he was a printer, Twain had the opportunity to read the stories he printed, and these stories introduced him to all types of writing.

At the age of twenty-two, Twain fulfilled his dream of working on the Mississippi River when he became a riverboat pilot. Twain also wrote for newspapers, lectured in foreign countries, and for a short time was a soldier in the Civil War. His first popular story, "The Celebrated Jumping Frog of Calaveras County," was published in 1865, when Twain was thirty years old.

Mark Twain's childhood adventures along the Mississippi River were the inspiration for two of his most famous books: *The Adventures of Tom Sawyer* and *The Adventures of Huckleberry Finn*. Other books written by Mark Twain include *The Prince and the Pauper*, *A Connecticut Yankee in King Arthur's Court*, and of course,

Personal Recollections of Joan of Arc. Millions of people have read and enjoyed Twain's stories, which have been translated into many languages and are still popular today.

Although he never completed his formal education, Twain was awarded honorary degrees by Yale University, Oxford University, and the University of Missouri. Mark Twain died in 1910 and is still recognized as one of the finest American writers.

Is there someone that you really admire? One person Mark Twain admired was the French heroine Joan of Arc. Twain thought Joan was one of the most amazing people who ever lived, and he was so inspired by her that he wrote PERSONAL RECOLLECTIONS OF JOAN OF ARC. Mark Twain once said he liked it best of all his books. I know you will like it too!

Mark Twain's book about Joan of Arc was published in 1896. The book tells the story of a young peasant girl who actually lived in France during the Middle Ages and was a true hero in the French battles against the English. *Personal Recollections of Joan of Arc*, which took Twain twelve years to research and write, has a lot of historical information about Joan and her life in 15th-century France.

However, *Personal Recollections of Joan of Arc* is not a history book. Twain tells the exciting story of Joan's life as *historical fiction*. This means Twain mixed history with his own imagination to tell his version of Joan's life. Many of the incidents in Twain's book really happened, and many of the characters he mentions really lived. Twain also created other characters to help tell Joan's story.

Mark Twain was known as a humorist, so people expected most of his books and stories to be funny. But because Twain admired the real Joan of Arc so much, he wanted people to take his book about her seriously. That is why he originally published *Personal Recollections of Joan of Arc* under a different name. That's right, he took *another* pen name! Twain created the character of Sieur Louis de Conte and listed him as the author of the book. While the real Joan of Arc did have a page named Louis, in Twain's book the character of Louis is Joan's best friend—and he is also the one who tells Joan's story. **I'm sniffing out a clue here! Louis's initials are S-L-C. Mark Twain is the pen name of Samuel Langhorne Clemens—S-L-C. Twain left a clue to the name of the real author for smart readers like us!**

Joan of Arc's story has inspired and influenced people like Mark Twain for over 500 years. Her story reminds us that one loyal and courageous person can change the course of history.

MAIN CHARACTERS

Joan of Arc—the great heroine

Louis de Conte (LOO-ee deh COHN)—Joan's best friend; later page and secretary to Joan

Father Fronte (FRON)—priest of Domrémy

Paladin (Pal-a-DAN)—Joan's childhood friend; later her standard-bearer

Charles VII—the future King of France, also known as the Dauphin (Doh-FAN)

General La Hire (lah HERE)—a general in the French army

Dwarf—Joan's man-at-arms

Bishop Cauchon (Coh-SHON)—questions Joan during the Great Trial

Manchon (Mahn-SHON)—records what was said during Great Trial

SETTING

Important Places

Domrémy (Dom-reh-MEE)—Joan's home village

Vaucouleurs (Voh-coo-LURE)—the city where Governor Baudricourt lives

Chinon (Shi-NON)—the city where the Dauphin's castle is located

Rheims (RHEHM)—the city where the King is crowned

Orléans (Or-lay-AHN)—the city of Joan's first battle

Paris—the city where an important battle takes place; where the English are most powerful

Rouen (Roo-AN)—the city of the Great Trial

Time Period

Joan of Arc takes place in the Middle Ages, during the Hundred Years' War. Joan was born in 1412 and lived during the final years of this long war. In fact, she is credited with helping to end it.

The Hundred Years' War was between England and France, and it began in 1337. This was a time when kings and queens ruled countries. Knights and nobles helped to command their battles, and many peasants fought the battles. When Joan of Arc was fighting in the war, she fought against two enemies: the English, because England wanted France's land; and other Frenchmen, because France was involved in a civil war. The French Duke of Burgundy and his supporters were fighting against the ruling royal family, King Charles VI and his heir, Charles VII. Because the Duke and the English wanted the same thing—to take power and land away from the rightful King—they fought together against Joan and her army.

1
A Passionate Deed

Do you have a special place? A place that is all your own? The children in the French village of Domrémy did. It was a big, beautiful beech tree. They believed tiny fairies lived in the tree, dancing in the leaves and between the branches. Some people in the village thought that the fairies were bad—especially Father Fronte (FRON), the local priest, who said that the fairies could stay in the tree as long as they didn't show themselves to people. Should they show themselves, the fairies would be banished, which meant they'd be asked to leave and find a new home.

Joan was very ill with a fever when the children of her village came running to her bed in a fury. They flew to her side, excited and fretting, crying out about the awful news.

"Joan, get up! You must get up! Oh, please, Joan, wake up or there will certainly be trouble," cried one of the children.

Still another child whimpered and sniffled as he tugged at the sleeve of Joan's nightshirt, pleading for her to answer.

"We haven't got very much time to save them," urged her dear friend Louis. "Joan, our fairy friends have been seen by Dame Aubrey, and she's been raving about it all day. Now Father Fronte has heard. You must talk to him. You're the only one who would know what to say to him."

Joan's body was weak and enflamed with fever; her mind was cloudy and she was unable to respond. As Louis and all the children realized that Joan could not help them, their hearts became very heavy. They wandered off, saddened that Father Fronte was surely going to banish the fairies, and they would lose their kind and caring friends.

And what affectionate and faithful friends the fairies were. The beautiful beech tree where they lived grew atop a velvety green mound, near a clear and peaceful spring. Joan, Louis, and all the children of the village would dance, sing, and cool themselves under the leafy shade of the tree during the summer. They believed their fairy playmates could scare away snakes and stinging insects and keep the spring fresh and full.

It was too late for the fairies, though. There was nothing the children could do now. By the end of the day, Father Fronte was already bringing his candles and incense and banners to their beloved tree. He marched around it and recited strange prayers, calling for the dear and gentle sprites to be banished.

The next day, when Joan was no longer feverish, the children came to her and told her the whole sad story. "Joan, Father Fronte has banished the fairies!" cried one little girl. "He says that our friends are more likely to be the friends of the devil than of children."

When Joan heard this, she became so angry that she flew from her bed to see Father Fronte. She thought that because of what he had done, the spring would no longer be fresh and the insects and snakes would return and multiply, bothering all those who visited the fairy tree. She felt it was a great tragedy for the children to lose their loving friends.

Louis and the other children, nervous with anticipation, scurried behind Joan as she went toward the parish house. She sailed through the door with the force of a strong wind and cried out, "Why have you taken from us our most trusted and loyal friends when they have proved to be such caring protectors? Why do you say they are friends of the devil? They have hurt no one for five hundred years."

Just as those words came out of her mouth, tears pooled in Joan's eyes. They were tears of frustration and sadness at the loss of her dear and loyal fairy friends.

"Please sit, my child. Let me explain," Father Fronte said with cool authority. "You must understand something. It was a sin for the fairies to show themselves."

Joan winced when she heard this explanation, and then her emotions rose. She ran into the priest's arms, crying, "How can you say that the fairies have sinned? The fairies committed no sin, for they did not know anyone was watching them."

"But this has been decreed, my child," said Father Fronte.

"Decreed by whom, and *why*?" exclaimed Joan.

"This is what has been passed down to me. If these beings, who are not of this earth, show themselves, they are to be banished," Father Fronte explained in a dull tone.

A decree is an order that has the force of law—in this case, the religious law of the time.

"The poor creatures did not know Dame Aubrey was watching them," Joan shouted as tears rolled down her cheeks. "Are they to be punished for something they did not know was wrong?"

When Father Fronte saw Joan's tears, he brought her close to his side, hugged her, and said, "There, there, don't cry. Nobody could be sorrier than I."

"But they are gone," cried Joan. "You have

banished the fairies forever. What you have done is no little matter. Is just being sorry enough?"

"Oh, dear child. You are right to accuse me," replied the Father. "Will it satisfy you if I wear ashes and a coarse sackcloth to show you my sorrow and repentance?"

"Yes," Joan answered calmly, no longer crying. "That will do."

Father Fronte was amused by Joan's seriousness. He turned his back as he walked to the fireplace, for it would have hurt Joan to see him laugh. Then he took a shovelful of cold ashes. He was about to empty them on his old gray head when a better idea came to him, and he said, "Would you mind helping me, Joan?"

"How, Father?"

He got down on his knees, bent his head low, and said, "Take the ashes and put them on my head for me."

As soon as Father Fronte uttered those words, Joan ran to his side and dropped to her knees.

"Oh, that is dreadful," cried Joan. "I did not know you meant to do this with the ashes. Please, Father, get up. I cannot bear to see you suffer."

"But I can't," said Father Fronte. "Not until I am forgiven. Do you forgive me? What can I do for your forgiveness?"

Joan pleaded, but Father Fronte would not get up

or put down the shovel filled with ashes. Then Joan had an idea. She seized the shovel.

"Th-there," she stammered as she poured the ashes over her own head. "It is done. Now please get up, Father."

Admiring Joan's courage and passion, Father Fronte gathered her in his arms and said, "Oh, you are such an extraordinary child! To make such a sacrifice! And all for what you believe in." Then he brushed the ashes out of Joan's hair and helped her clean her face and neck.

2
Joan the Brave

Joan, Louis, and all the other children of the village were growing up fast. The Hundred Years' War between England and France had been raging for a long time, and England was always hungry for more French land. With battles going on all the time to the north and west of their village, the children grew more and more patriotic every day.

The sun was low and the hills surrounding Joan's home were quiet. It was the time of day when the villagers gathered at their tables for their evening meal. They'd talk of news, play games, tell tales or fortunes, or just complain.

As he so often did, Louis joined Joan and her family for dinner. Joan's house was like a second home to him. His parents had been killed by the English and he was an orphan. Father Fronte, who lived in the church next door to Joan's house, raised and cared for him. He taught Louis to read and write—skills few children in Domrémy had.

It wasn't unusual at this time of day for a person to knock at a stranger's door, hoping a generous family would share their meal. On this wintry evening, a beggar walking by Joan's home inhaled the aroma of cooking food as it drifted out the windows. He stopped and knocked on the door.

The poor beggar was let in. He stamped his wet feet, brushed the wetness from his coat, and took off his limp hat, slapping it against his leg to knock off the snow. Then he glanced around the room with a hungry look in his eyes.

"What a blessed thing to have a fire to warm you, a roof overhead, loving friends to talk with—and, yes, rich food to eat," said the beggar as his eyes fell on the bowls of food in everyone's hands. "God help the homeless who must trudge the roads in this weather." He stood there smiling, appealing to one face after the other, but his smile faded as he realized that he was not welcome.

Joan and Louis, sitting by the fire, looked into each others eyes with both worry and surprise. Then Joan rose and began walking toward the beggar.

"Sit down! Do you hear me? Sit down, I say!" commanded Joan's father.

"But Father, the man is hungry. I'm sure he has not eaten a meal in a long while, and with the winds in his face day and night, I'm sure he must need—"

"Need! If you have need, you work," said her father sternly. "Let him find work, and then he will have food."

"Father, if you tell me not to feed the poor man, then I won't," Joan replied. "But why punish him? It is not his fault that food and work are scarce."

"I'm not going to feed every ragged straggler that passes my door," continued her father. "We are being eaten out of house and home.... Anyway, he has the face of a rascal."

"I know not if he is a rascal, Father," said Joan. "But he is hungry, and I would like to give him my porridge—I do not need it."

"Rascals should not have help from honest people. I will not have it. If you do not obey me..."

Joan's father went on and on, with words and arguments pouring out from him. He paced and waved his arms. Others in the room joined in, arguing for and against feeding the hungry man. Finally Joan's father changed his mind.

"All right, Joan—give him the food!" he shouted above all the voices.

Joan was embarrassed and did not know what to say. While her father was busy arguing, she had already given the man her porridge.

"Why did you not wait for my decision, daughter?" asked her scowling father.

"Father, the man's stomach was very hungry

She has a point. An empty stomach is an unhappy stomach.

and it would not have been wise to wait," Joan explained.

The poor homeless man, with his thin face and tattered clothes, was already finishing off the meal. After a while, with his stomach warm and full, he began to talk.

"I have been among the soldiers in this awful war that is upon France," he began. "They bravely fight the English, but the strength of our French patriots is fading, and one by one I have seen them fall."

The man went on with his stories, and they awakened everyone's love for France. Joan's father sat by the fireplace listening. His face gleamed and his eyes were wide with pride for his country. Joan's and Louis's hearts thumped as the exciting stories unfolded.

The beggar finished his last story, and tears filled his eyes as he rose to leave. But before he moved to the door, he went to Joan. He touched his weak hand to her head and said, "Thank you so much, my child. I was near death, and you have brought me back to life."

Joan looked up into his tearful eyes.

"Now listen, my child," he said. "Here is your reward."

And then, from this weary man, a beautiful voice was heard. The grateful stranger began to sing. It was the most noble and stirring song a French audience could hear. From his lips came the great *Song of Roland*, France's most patriotic song of the time. **As legend tells us, Roland was a great French hero. He died in battle, and this song honors his brave deeds. It was as heartfelt and famous in Joan's time as our GOD BLESS AMERICA is today.**

By the time the stranger finished singing, everyone's eyes had filled with tears. They were proud to be French and felt love for their country—and this gentle man. Joan was the first one to go to him. She hugged the stranger as though she had known him all her life.

The winter passed slowly, but then gentle spring breezes began to blow and sweet flowery scents filled the air. By then Joan was ten years old, and she had grown into a lovely young girl. Her friends in the village had given her the nickname "Beautiful." She was also called "Bashful," for the easy flush of red that came to her cheeks around strangers; "Patriot," because her feelings for her country were so strong; and even "Brave," the name the children gave her one unusual day.

On this day, as they often did, Joan and Louis went to the fairy tree. There they joined the village children. The air was clear, the spring was quiet, and the light on the horizon was rosy and warm. It was dusk, and the tree looked especially enchanting at that time. All the children were playing, singing, or hanging garlands of flowers in memory of their lost fairy friends. Suddenly someone cried out.

"*Look, look!* Over there!" A little girl was pointing frantically. "Down the slope, toward the village. It's a black flag!"

"What does it mean?" asked a young boy called Paladin (Pal-a-DAN).

Louis knew what it meant. And Joan's face gave it away in a minute. She bore her pained expression without uttering a word. All her youthful hopes were drained from her at the very moment that she saw the dreadful banner flapping in the wild wind. **Woe! A black flag meant that bad news was on the way.**

All of the children except Joan ran to the approaching flagbearer. "I'm sure I do not have happy news, my little friends," he announced when he reached the tree.

Most of the children chattered anxiously. Joan and Louis, however, looked at each other with worried frowns.

"France will have no flag now," continued the boy. "The English have signed a treaty with King Charles VI. The treaty says his son, Charles VII, who is the rightful heir to the French throne, will not be crowned. The treaty appoints an English heir instead, so when King Charles VI dies, we will be ruled by the English!"

"An *Englishman* will wear the crown and rule France?" cried Paladin. "It is a lie! What will become of our Dauphin?" **"Dauphin" was a nickname given to the eldest son of the French King—the son who was next in line to become King. In this case, it was Charles VII.**

Sobs and gasps burst from the children as they

realized that France would be controlled by the English. There was an uproar—everybody talking at once. Joan became pale and did not say a word. Her elder brother, Jacques, put his hand on her head to comfort her, and Joan gathered his hand to her lips and kissed it for thanks.

Then Paladin spoke. "Are we never going to become men?" he asked in an accusing tone. "France needs us. Do we allow our country to finally fall to the greedy English because we may seem too young to fight a war?"

"We've always got to wait and wait," another boy chimed in. "We never get a chance.... If only I could be a soldier now!"

"As for me, I'm not going to wait much longer," said Paladin.

"Neither will I," yelled one boy after the other.

"And when I'm a soldier," Paladin bragged, "you'll hear from me, I promise you. I will not ride in the rear. I will be at the front with the officers when we storm the fortresses!"

Even the girls caught the boys' spirit. "If I were a man, I would start this minute!" said one girl. She looked very proud of herself and glanced around for applause.

"So would I," another girl added.

"Pooh!" said Paladin. "*Girls.* They can brag, but that is all they are good for. Let them come face to face

with soldiers if you want to see what running is like...."
Paladin trailed off for a moment as he considered one
more point. "And little Joan—next *she'll* tell us she will
become a soldier!"

The idea was so funny that it got a good laugh
from some of the boys, which gave Paladin a little
more encouragement.

"Why, can you just see her?" crowed Paladin.
"No, no, not a common soldier, a captain yet. Yes,
there she is right before you in her heavy armor,
leading an army of a hundred men!" Then Paladin
laughed so hard his sides ached.

Joan faced Paladin as he mocked her. He was still
laughing when Joan suddenly turned toward the fairy
tree, which she could see from the corner of her eye.

A strange man was standing behind the tree,
turning his head this way and that and waving his
arms wildly. The glare from the setting sun made it
difficult to see who it was. The man came out from
behind the dark tree trunk, frantically waving a huge
axe in the air. It was Ben, the madman who for years
had lived in a cage in the village so he couldn't hurt
anyone. Many of the children shrieked as they ran to
hide behind distant bushes or boulders. Paladin ran
the farthest, dashing for the spring and leaping from
stone to stone to cross to the far side.

While the other children ran away, Joan calmly
walked toward Ben as he continued to wobble toward

her, still cutting through the air with his axe. He threatened her with the weapon, but Joan spoke to him in a calm and gentle voice.

Louis, Joan's closest friend, called out with alarm from behind a wide bush. *"Joan! Over here! Don't be crazy. Get over here!"* Then he covered his eyes with his hands as the axe was about to come down on Joan's head.

When Louis could finally stand to look up again, what he saw shocked him. The axe was lying on the ground where Joan and Ben had stood, and Joan was walking with the madman, hand in hand, in the direction of the village. **Wow! And how do you suppose she managed that?**

One by one the boys and girls came out from their hiding places and gathered under the tree again. They were gazing in awe with their mouths open, watching Joan and the madman walk down the hill.

Then the children started back to town. When they arrived there, they found that Ben had been brought back to his cage. Many villagers were excited by the news and gathered in the square. The women hugged and kissed Joan and praised her for her deed. The men patted her on the head and said that if she were a man, they would send her to war and never doubt that she would be a good soldier. Joan was very modest and was embarrassed by the attention. She tore herself away and found Louis. Together they returned to the fairy tree, where they sat quietly and watched as the last bit of sun set behind the distant hills.

The other children remained in the square, standing off to the side. They were all silent and thinking the same thing—that they were cowards compared to Joan. When people asked them what they had done, they tried to give all types of explanations to hide their cowardice. Paladin spoke the loudest and went on the longest.

"Oh, pooh!" he said. "You'd think that it was heroic for Joan to stand up to such a feeble man. Why, it is nothing! If he was to come along now, I wouldn't care if he had a *thousand* axes. I would walk up to him and I would say..."

And he went on and on, telling the brave things that he would say and do. Other children put in a word from time to time, but in the end they all agreed that Joan had done something extraordinary. And it was then that they gave Joan her other nickname— Joan the Brave.

So little Joan of Arc performed her first brave deed at the age of ten! That's seventy in dog years, but for a person, that's pretty young! The villagers of Domrémy realized that Joan was special, but they couldn't guess what the young girl would eventually do for them—and for all of France!

3
The War at Home

Years passed and Joan grew into a graceful girl of sixteen. In her face there was a sweetness and purity that reflected her spiritual nature. Those years were pretty good ones in Domrémy. The current King, Charles VI, had died. The war was still on, but it had not yet come to Domrémy. One day, though, Joan saw firsthand how awful the war with the English really was.

"We don't have enough time, Louis!" Joan screamed up from the bottom stair. "*Hurry!* The smoke is getting too thick. Get yourself down here—the English are getting closer!"

"When did they get here?" Louis breathlessly asked as he jumped out of bed.

"They came at the darkest hour of the night, those English beasts. I barely had enough time to get my clothes because the house was burning so quickly. They have already destroyed so much." Joan's voice was calm and even as she conveyed the awful news. Louis was ashamed to feel the panic that was filling him as they marched quickly away from the village.

"My brothers Pierre and Jean wouldn't stop trying to put out the fire that was spreading across our thatched roof," Joan continued. "Finally they realized that they'd better run or they would die. My parents and the rest of the village escaped through the oak woods."

Soon Joan and Louis caught up with the others. Many villagers were whimpering and crying, but Joan was patient and clearheaded, and she took command.

"Everyone, walk calmly to the woods and find cover until morning," she said with easy authority. "At that time, I will go back toward the village to see if we can return—or if we must continue on to the next town."

Louis admired Joan as she finished speaking. He was surprised to see that the villagers did not object to her decisions. They listened, and then they did as she said. Joan had brought such calm to all the chaos that the townspeople were glad to have her take charge.

When dawn came, Joan returned with news that everyone could go back to their homes. But this was a mixed blessing. A considerable part of the town had been burned.

When the villagers reached the square, they saw smoke-blackened homes and stores. In the alleys, they saw slaughtered animals of every kind. But the most horrifying sight was yet to come. Louis was sickened by it, and he was relieved that he made the dreadful discovery before Joan did.

"Joan, don't come over here," he called from down the lane.

"What are you hiding from me, Louis? Do you think that I am not already pained by what I see?" She was getting closer, and there was nothing Louis could do to stop her. "Louis..."

Joan's voice trailed off as she saw Ben the madman lying in a corner of his cage, lifeless and bloody. She put her face in her hands and cried. Then, with her head still in her hands, she sadly said, "Is life so harsh? It is so unfair that such things can happen to those who are so helpless and innocent."

Joan had never seen such violence or witnessed such a dreadful sight. She turned away in horror and would not come any closer. She stood for a moment more, raised her head, and then walked off.

Louis had never seen such violence either. Both he and Joan were deeply saddened by it. Once the sadness lessened, however, Joan began talking about this terrible event. She became more and more troubled by the injustices of the war.

4
A Girl
Becomes a Knight

"Louis," Joan uttered. "Come to the tree with me."

When the two were seated beneath the great beech tree, Joan began to speak in a strangely quiet and even tone.

"I cannot bear to see the death of the French people, nor tolerate living under English rule. Our suffering and pain must end. We must fight the English."

Joan continued to speak as though she were in a trance. Louis had heard her speak like this before. He had seen the same absent and distant look she now had on her face. But never before had she said something so outrageous.

"How? We have no soldiers to fight with!" Louis exclaimed.

"*We* will be soldiers. And France will rise again. You shall see."

"Rise? With the English armies everywhere in France? What army will we join? There are nearly none left. Most have been trampled or frightened off. How do you know such things, Joan? You speak as though you know the future."

"My voices have told me these things," she said as she looked her loyal friend in the eyes.

"Voices! What voices, Joan?"

"My voices. They have never told me lies. They have told me that *I* am to form an army."

"You, Joan? You, form an army? And *whose* voice has sent you to carry out this impossible task?"

"It is God. He will help me. I am told that I will lead His armies and win back France. Our true King, the Dauphin, will be crowned and proclaimed as the one and only leader of France.

"Tomorrow I will go to Robert de Baudricourt (BOW-dree-core), the governor of Vaucouleurs (Voh-coo-LURE). He will give me men-at-arms for an escort and send me to the Dauphin." **Remember that the English had signed a treaty with the King of France that said the next ruler of France would be an Englishman—not the Dauphin.**

Louis believed the things Joan said to him. He didn't know why—he only knew that in his heart they rang true. His mind doubted, but his heart believed. The authority of Joan's voice and the greatness of her heart had filled him with patriotism and faith.

Then Joan lowered her head. She began to cry. When she was calm, she spoke again. "Oh, Louis, I am so young. So young to leave my mother and my home and go out into the strange world to do something so great. How can I go to the war—and lead armies? I, a girl, and ignorant of such things, knowing nothing of arms, nor how to mount a horse, nor ride it.... Yet, if it is commanded..."

Joan's voice sank a little and was broken by sobs. Louis sat by silently and hugged her. He knew that he was witnessing something mysterious—something that only Joan could understand.

Soon after, Joan led a group north to meet the governor. They were a small band of youngsters: Louis, and Joan's younger brothers Pierre and Jean were the only ones who pledged to follow Joan. It was a day's journey from their village to Vaucouleurs, and they arrived at the castle the next day at noon. They were taken to the dining hall, where Joan faced the governor and several of his guests. She, a simple peasant girl, stood before the nobles and mighty men and spoke what was in her heart.

Sometimes it's hard to remember that Joan is just a kid! And a pretty brave one too....

"I have come, Your Excellency, to ask of you an army." Joan was steady and erect as she stood before the governor.

This strange speech amazed the governor and his company, and a murmur rose in the audience. In the midst of this stir, the governor spoke.

"You poor child, are you mad? Leave me in peace to eat my meal with my guests."

Joan did not move, but she continued to make

39

her demands known. "Please, sir, give me an escort of men-at-arms and send me to the Dauphin. The Lord has sent me to you because you are a wise and just man. I am to drive the English out of France and crown the Dauphin the King of France. This is what the Lord has put in my heart, and I must follow."

All around, Joan could hear people murmuring, "Poor thing. The poor thing has lost her mind." Louis began to worry that they would take her away in chains. While the crowd was making fun of her, Joan continued to speak with authority.

"Your Excellency, already another battle has been lost today. The French army will suffer even greater losses if you do not send me to the Dauphin soon."

"How can you know that the battle has been lost today? It would take eight or ten days for word of that event to arrive!" **There were no phones or fax machines in France back then. Messages were delivered by people on horseback who sometimes had to travel many days through a war-torn country. Not my idea of fun.**

"God has brought the news to me," Joan calmly replied.

The confused governor began to pace across the dining room floor. He muttered to himself and his eyes darted this way and that. Then he said, "If I receive word that such an event has truly taken place, I will give you a letter and send you to see the Dauphin."

"You will fetch me in nine days, Your Excellency,"

were Joan's last prophetic words. She led her friends back to their village, where they were to wait out the remainder of the nine days. **"Prophetic" comes from the word "prophecy." It means telling the future. Joan is predicting that the governor will get his news and send her to the Dauphin in nine days.**

On the ninth day, the governor came with his guards and torchbearers. He delivered to Joan a mounted escort, horses, and equipment for Louis and her brothers. From the crowd, the governor pulled a handful of men to make a small army. Among these soldiers were men who had just returned from battle. Others were villagers who had simply come to see the spectacle—one of which was the very reluctant Paladin, Joan's childhood friend.

Joan was raised onto a sleek black horse and handed the letter for the Dauphin. Then from atop his own horse, the governor leaned over, took off his sword, belted it around Joan's waist with his own hands, and said in awe, "What you said was true, child. The battle was lost. I believe now that you were sent from God. My sword is yours. This weapon is a symbol of peace that can only be won through war."

Joan led the small group in double file out of their beloved town. Her parents and all the villagers watched with wonder as an army of twenty-five soldiers and knights were led by a stately black horse, upon which sat the patriotic crusader, Joan of Arc.

Joan's young face glowed. She sat proudly on her beautiful horse, with her chest high and her eyes wide. And her heart was filled with love for her country and hope for peace.

Joan was on her way to the Dauphin's castle in Chinon (Shi-NON) with good news. She would drive the English out of France and have the Dauphin crowned the King of France. But did anyone believe a young country girl could do that? We'll see!

5
Doubters and Tricksters

Joan and the governor's escort had been riding for days, and some of the men had never even been on a horse before. They were getting restless and mean. Joan had to have loyal men who would follow her and believe in what she was doing. She needed to do something...and soon.

"I will have no more of this," Joan called out to her troop when they stopped to camp for the night. All day Joan had been listening to a chorus of moans, groans, and curses, which floated up the ranks to her position at the head of the troop. She had heard enough.

"Conduct yourselves like noble guards and men-at-arms, as you should. Otherwise, how will you defend anyone, even yourselves? I will not hear of your weak limbs and tired heads anymore!" she said.

"She is right," Paladin whispered to Louis, "for last night I heard some men whine, wail, and swear, saying their saddles were hard and they wished they hadn't been chosen by the governor."

"The voice you heard last night was your own," replied Louis.

"The saddle didn't hurt me!" boasted Paladin. "I don't see how they could talk like that. Pooh! I was born in a saddle...and yet this was the first time I was ever on a horse! All the old soldiers admired my riding. They said they'd never seen anything like it...."

Louis was getting restless listening to Paladin's bragging. He knew Paladin was stretching the truth again. It was Paladin who had trouble staying on his horse. Then Louis's ears perked up when he heard the last of Joan's announcement over Paladin's whispers. "Maybe what we need is to put you through some horsemanship drills!" Then Joan ordered drills for the youngest soldiers, who had the least experience riding. The drills began immediately.

"These exercises are refreshing," Paladin quietly remarked to Louis, "but I didn't need them. I've joined in just to show Joan and the others what a willing soldier I am."

Louis, unimpressed, nodded and laughed as Paladin continued to struggle with the exercises. Joan complimented all the men as they worked on the drills, and their confidence grew—even Paladin's.

As the march continued, the soldiers became weary and uncomfortable. They had ridden through prickly bushes and crossed wide, frigid streams. Afterward, while still wet, they slept on frosty, snowy ground. They were weakening, and some were resentful of their determined leader. One frustrated soldier spoke up when he and a small group were sitting alone in the camp:

"What is this leader, this *girl*? Is she human? She never tires."

"She is always alert and strong, while we are limping like beaten children," added a soldier who was lying on the ground with his eyes closed and his head resting on a rock.

Then he and the rest of the resentful soldiers began to argue. Some said that it was Joan's youthfulness that allowed her to be tireless. But others said that she was too strange and that she must be a witch who gained her strength from witchcraft. They made a plan to take her life when the right moment came.

Two of Joan's knights overheard these betrayers and told Joan, urging her to hang the plotters. But Joan was not disturbed by this news.

"No, I could not take these men's lives. But they will soon learn that their plottings and doubts will not help them," Joan said confidently. "Call them before me."

Joan addressed the ringleader when the group stood before her. "It is a pity that you should plot another's death when your own is so close at hand."

All the men were astonished by her claim. The ringleader was very frightened because Joan spoke with such confidence.

The next day, when the troop was crossing the river, the ringleader's horse stumbled and fell on him.

He was drowned in the rough waters before anyone could get to him. Joan's prophecy had come true.

After that, there were no more grumblings and complaints from the men. They now realized that Joan knew things that they could never know. They began to believe that Joan was their true leader.

The following day, in the rain, the small army filed out from the dense forest. Joan had always ridden at the head of the column of soldiers, and that was where she took her post now. They rode for three or four miles when the rain turned to sleet. It lashed against the soldiers' faces. Louis, who rode very near to Joan, envied his good friend, who wore a helmet with a visor that protected her face from the sleet.

Suddenly a harsh voice came out of the darkness. "Halt! Well, you have taken your time, Captain Raymond," said a man who rode up next to Joan. "And what have you found out? Is she still behind us?"

Joan realized that the soldier did not know who she was. She lowered her voice and said, "She is still behind. I have seen her."

"Good!" said this strange horseman. "I was afraid she might be ahead of us. Now that we know that she is behind us, everything is safe."

Joan and all who were near her, including Louis, prayed silently to themselves that Joan's true identity would not be revealed to this confused soldier. Louis and some of the others were certainly frightened, but

Joan was not. Her heart was calm and her mind was alert. She had quickly found a solution—she pretended to be this man, Captain Raymond.

"Everyone has heard of this Joan of Arc," the soldier continued. "And people are speaking of this *girl's* power. It was said in Vaucouleurs that she went before the governor and told him that she heard God's voice. She is a witch! She does not hear God's voice. She uses spells to get what she wants! We will trap her and then we will hang her."

Joan spoke again, using her deepest voice. "They might use the bridge ahead as an escape. With your permission, I will go and destroy it."

"Good idea. You have it, Captain, and my thanks," said the unidentified soldier, and then he saluted and was on his way.

"Forward!" Joan commanded, hiding her great relief.

The troop moved on. Joan gave another command, and the soldiers quickly made their way to the river, crossed it, and then burned the bridge behind them.

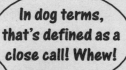

In dog terms, that's defined as a close call! Whew!

Louis rode with a broad smile on his face as he thought of Joan. She was becoming a great leader. When he got the chance, he rode up beside Joan's horse.

"Joan, you are so clever. No, in fact, you are brilliant!" Louis could hardly control his amazement. Joan, modest as she was, smiled and blushed. Then she turned her horse to continue the march.

Before this incident, the men were reluctant to march in the gloom and silence of dark, dense forests. But now their reluctance faded as they realized what a smart soldier Joan was. All of Joan's men—her brothers, Paladin, the knights, and the guards—rode alongside their wise leader, feeling a renewed strength and purpose.

A few days before they reached Chinon, the troop stopped in a small village to refresh and replenish their food. Joan called for Louis.

"Yes, Joan?" Louis said cheerfully as he approached her. "What can I do for you?" Louis was always happy when Joan called him for a private meeting.

"I must dictate a letter to you for the Dauphin. I will send my knights ahead with the letter, informing him of our purpose and our arrival," she said, and then Joan began to dictate to Louis:

I have come hundreds of miles to bring you good news, Your Excellency. I beg the privilege of delivering this news in person. Although I have never seen you, I am sure I will know you even if you are in disguise.

The next day the knights took Joan's letter to the Dauphin. They returned with the news that the Dauphin would not see her.

"The Dauphin's advisers are traitors to France, and they scheme for their own selfish rewards," said one of the knights. "They told the Dauphin not to see you, Joan." She was very sad to receive this news. **These advisers fear Joan's influence over the Dauphin, because up to this point no one has interfered with the advice that they alone give him.**

Luckily for Joan, there was someone who was even closer to the Dauphin than his advisers—his mother-in-law, Queen Yolande. When she heard of Joan's letter, she took it from the advisers and approached her son-in-law when they were alone.

"Charles, I think you *should* see this girl. She is too amazing to be ignored."

"My advisers think that the voices she hears may not be from God," he replied. "They think she may be a witch."

"A child who has accomplished so much could only receive this courage and direction from God," explained the Queen. "I believe you must see her face to face and decide for yourself."

The Dauphin called Joan's knights back. They told the Dauphin of Joan's pure and beautiful character, and how she had outwitted the murderous soldier they met on the way to Chinon. The Dauphin was very impressed, and he was convinced to see Joan. The knights returned to Joan with the happy news.

When Joan arrived at the castle in Chinon, it was filled with a lavish procession of servants—something she had never seen before. At the entrance to the castle stood four heralds in royal red and gold uniforms, and music blew from their slender silver trumpets. Inside the castle, silk banners and rich tapestries hung from the walls. Joan, Louis, and her knights moved down the aisle to the throne. The trumpets sounded every fifty feet. Joan and her knights were proud and happy, and they held themselves erect like the fine soldiers they were. As they approached the throne, Joan stepped ahead and bowed—but not toward the throne. **What is she doing? This is the future King of France. Joan is usually so respectful....**

"God of his grace, give you long life, dear and gentle Dauphin," she said as she raised her head and looked toward a simply dressed young man standing in the crowd beside the throne.

"Ah, you have made a mistake, my child. I am not the Dauphin. There he is." The man pointed to the throne.

Louis immediately understood what was happening. The Dauphin had taken Joan up on the strange promise made in her letter—that she could identify him even in disguise. Louis smiled. He felt confident that Joan would do the right thing.

Joan did not waver. She still held her face toward

the Dauphin, and said, "No, gracious one. You are he, and none other."

It was a miracle. All who were present were stunned that Joan could identify the Dauphin. His amazement was visible too.

"But tell me, child, who are you, and why have you come to see me?"

"I am Joan of Arc, and I am sent to you to say that God, the King in Heaven, wills that you be crowned King of France. He also wills that you give me an army for my appointed work, which is to drive the English out of France."

"Off with you," the Dauphin called to his attendants. "I would like to speak with this young girl in private." With a wave of his hand, all the people moved to the other side of the hall.

"How can I be sure that what you say is true?" the Dauphin asked Joan. "You are so young and have little experience as a soldier."

"I will give you a sign, and you shall have no more doubts. I know things that no one else knows— that only God could know," Joan announced boldly. "There is a secret in your heart that has troubled you for a long time."

Charles was quiet and breathless as he waited to hear what she knew.

"You *are* the lawful heir to France and the true heir to the throne. You *must not* doubt your birthright."

The Dauphin was shocked. He had always feared that he would not be considered the legitimate King and that laws would rob him of the throne if he ever gained it. Because of these doubts, he had fought weakly against the English all these years.

"You have revealed my deepest secret. I feel now that you truly speak for God," he proclaimed. "I will give you the army that you request. You must rid the roads and towns of the English and reclaim our land for France."

"Your Excellency, that is my plan," replied Joan. "I will march to Orléans with the army you give me. The English have control of all the fortresses and the land around the city. To win at Orléans will give us a great advantage over the English. Then you will be crowned King and begin your absolute rule over all of France!"

Hard to believe, isn't it? Joan of Arc, a seventeen-year-old girl who couldn't read or write, wanted the Dauphin to give her an army to fight for France. Remember back at Vaucouleurs? Everyone thought Joan was crazy. Some said she was a witch! But look how far she got! And just wait till you see how far she's going to go....

6
Questions, Questions, and More Questions

Joan was ready to take her army into the French countryside to fight for France. But the Dauphin's advisers would not allow her to leave yet. They continued to discuss Joan with the Dauphin.

"Your Highness." One of the advisers approached Charles at his throne. "Joan of Arc says that she hears voices. And she has told you that those voices come from God.... Is this correct?"

"Yes, yes. That is what she has told me, and she has also told me something that only I could know," he replied.

The adviser, a small, thin man with a narrow chin and sharp eyes, continued with his intruding questions. "You say a secret known only to yourself and God?"

"That's right. And when Joan knew my secret, my doubts about her were cleared away," the Dauphin explained.

"But Your Excellency," the adviser said in a slow,

gravelly voice. "How do you know she has been sent by God? Maybe she is a witch. **Oh, no! Not again!** Witches can also know secrets in a person's soul—but *they* will use them to destroy you. It is dangerous to simply accept what Joan says as truth."

That was all Charles had to hear. His belief in Joan shriveled up like a raisin. He appointed a group of bishops to determine if Joan was sent by God. **Bishops are religious leaders who make important decisions. The Dauphin called them because they had the authority to validate Joan's claims.**

Every day Joan was called before the bishops, who questioned her about her mission and the divine guidance she received. They finally concluded that they couldn't tell whether or not Joan was sent by God. They recommended that the Dauphin send for a more experienced group of men from the university— scholars who had studied religion and law and were better trained to ask the necessary questions. These men were also known as *inquisitors*. **Joan lived in the Middle Ages, during a period in history called the Inquisition. People were always being questioned about their religious beliefs, and inquisitors were the officials who asked the questions.** Joan was called before them. She asked Louis to go with her in case there was something she had to read.

"You say that God has told you to save France from the English?" one of the scholars asked Joan.

"Yes. He has told me many times," Joan said proudly.

"You have asked the Dauphin for an army so that you can fight the English?" the inquisitor continued.

Joan thought carefully about the question before she answered.

"Yes. I *have* asked for an army.... And the sooner I have it, the better," she said defiantly.

The inquisitor was impressed with Joan's confidence, and he decided to change the subject. "You say God speaks to you. Show us how this is done."

Joan was fierce with her response. "I have not come here to show you miracles. I have come here to fight for France. Give me my army and send me on my mission! Then you will hear of miracles, and you will know that what I do is God's will."

Helllooo! Start flipping the book pages and check out the action . . . . Woo-cha!

Day after day, Joan was asked more questions. Day after day, she answered with dignity and respect. Then, after three weeks, all the men from the university came to a decision.

Everyone rose as one of the inquisitors made a speech. "It is found, and is hereby declared, that Joan of Arc is a good Christian. There is nothing that she has said that is contrary to good faith. Charles should accept her mission and give her the army she requested. And furthermore, the Church will permit Joan to dress like a man." **Well, we haven't heard about this before! Obviously, a girl wearing men's clothing was unusual. However, the scholars decided that if Joan must do the work of a man and a soldier, she should dress for the job.**

Couriers were sent to inform the Dauphin of the decision. Soon after he was told, bugles were heard in Chinon. This meant that there would be an announcement from the Dauphin.

When all the citizens reached the town square, they found the herald atop a pedestal. Joan and Louis were nearby as the herald began his proclamation in a powerful voice. "Know all, fellow citizens, that the high, the most illustrious Dauphin, by the grace of God the rightful King of France, is pleased to give Joan of Arc, the Maid, the title and authority of General-in-Chief of the Armies of France."

With a renewed spirit of hope, hundreds of townspeople threw their caps into the air, and the people cheered. Then the herald continued, "She will be given an army and attendants from the royal house, and she shall have the great General La Hire by her side."

The crowd roared again, thrilled to know that

France would be protected by an army led by the divinely inspired Joan of Arc and the great war hero General La Hire. All the lanes around the square began to fill with people dancing and cheering.

Soon people all over France heard about Joan the Maid and her army. From that day on, people sought out Joan's company so that they could be in her presence. They felt Joan's courage and faith and knew she was close to God. Joan had awakened the people of France from their defeated ways. With the renewed spirit to defend their country, they were eager to enlist in Joan's army. Thousands joined from Chinon, from Vaucouleurs—from all parts of France, men came to join the ranks of France's new army, led by Joan of Arc.

During the next few weeks, the Dauphin made sure that Joan and her army were equipped as a royal army should be. They were provided with new armor, and the Dauphin's tailors made them beautiful new uniforms.

When the army was ready to march out of Chinon, Joan, Louis, Joan's brothers Jean and Pierre, Paladin, and General La Hire were at the head of the vast army. Next in line was a group of priests carrying a banner of the Cross, which flew in the wind above their heads. The army was splendid to look at. The soldiers wore uniforms that were the colors of the sunset—blazing reds and golds. And they donned plumes on their headgear and red sashes across their chests. Joan's armor was especially brilliant. It was made of the finest steel, plated with silver, and decorated with engraved designs.

As the crowd cheered for their new leader, Joan bowed her plumed head to the left and right and began to ride forward. Her mounted soldiers, numbering in the thousands, followed in double file. They moved through the narrow streets of the town and past the castle. The townspeople followed them, singing and dancing.

They were marching to their first battle to rid France of the English invaders. And as the war songs and thunderous drums filled the air, the men and their great leader, the teenage Joan of Arc, sat higher on their horses—proud to represent Charles, France, and God.

Wow! I'm dizzy just thinking about how far Joan has come since she left Domrémy—and she's only seventeen. Just a short time ago she was a peasant girl living in a small country village. Now everyone has heard of her. In fact, everywhere she rides with her army, she is greeted with cheers. It certainly seems that she's won the hearts of the people of France...or has she?

7

Nothing Is Impossible

Well, Joan and her army were finally heading toward their first battle: a very famous one—the Battle of Orléans! Joan chose this as her first battle because it was the mission that God told her to follow—and it would help win the war against the English. But before her army marched to Orléans, she had to prepare them for the difficult times ahead.

The army had been traveling for days toward the city of Orléans. They rode through a forest until Joan led them out into a clearing. From there she could see in the distance a stone wall and the gate to a town. Joan raised her arm above her head.

"Halt!" yelled La Hire as soon as Joan made the signal.

"Halt!...Halt!...Halt!..." The command got fainter and fainter as it was carried back into the massive army riding behind.

"We will stop here for a few hours," Joan announced.

General La Hire was confused. He knew that this was not Orléans and that the English did not have soldiers in this small village. But he did not question this. He knew he should follow Joan's orders.

Joan and Louis rode off toward the village gate, leaving La Hire and the army to rest on the open road. When she came to the gate, Joan rode through the town as if she knew where she was going. God had sent her to this village, and she was confident that He would lead her to St. Catherine's chapel. Louis followed. When they reached the chapel, Joan got down from her horse, went to the door, and knocked. A priest answered.

"Good day, Father." Joan spoke gently, with a calm yet powerful certainty. "Pardon me, but I have come to your chapel to visit the altar of St. Catherine. Our Father in Heaven has directed me here."

The priest was surprised to see a woman dressed as a soldier.

"I have come to claim the ancient sword that is buried there," she continued.

"I do not know of such a sword. Are you sure you have come to the right place?" the priest asked with a raised brow as he nervously fingered the rope belt around his cloak.

"Yes. I am quite sure, Father. I am told that it is buried under the ground behind the altar," Joan confirmed. "May we go to the shrine now?"

The priest gestured with a small, doubtful nod for Joan and Louis to come into the chapel. Then he

guided them to the shrine. Joan went behind the altar and bent down as Louis and the priest watched.

They were amazed to see that Joan was on her knees, picking out the dirt between the old stones that paved the floor around the shrine. Then she removed three or four stones, and there it appeared. The metal hilt of the sword was sticking up just above the surface dirt.

Joan removed more stones and dug up the sword. When she pulled it out, it was covered with rust, which she rubbed away. The priest was shocked that this young soldier had uncovered a sword in his chapel.

Joan turned to the priest and Louis to explain. "This is a sacred sword. God has led me here because this sword was used hundreds of years ago by a great French patriot. And now with the Lord's divine authority, I will take it to battle for France once again."

"If you can wait, I would like to clean and polish it. That is the least I can do for you," the priest said. "And I'd better sharpen it as well."

"It is not necessary to sharpen it," Joan replied quickly. "That old blade will be fine. It is not my mission to kill anyone. I will only carry it as a symbol of authority."

The priest smiled warmly and went to clean the sword. Meanwhile, Joan and Louis returned to the army waiting outside the village. Joan led them up to the town wall. When they came to the gate, Joan stopped to await the priest. He came out shortly and presented the beautiful, shiny silver sword. Joan took the sword by the hilt and waved it in the air. The army cheered.

"Forward!" she yelled, and the army marched on toward Orléans.

When the sun had finally gone down below the trees on the horizon, the army camped for the night. Everyone was tired and hungry, and they were relieved to be able to eat and rest. Louis, Joan's brothers, and Paladin were gathered near their tents when Joan approached them.

It had been a while since Joan was able to join her dear old friends. But this was an official visit. Joan had to appoint people to her private staff. **As General-in-Chief of the army, Joan had her own private staff—a group of soldiers attendant to Joan's personal care before and during battles. These included a page to deliver messages and assist Joan with anything she needed, a secretary to write Joan's letters, and a standard-bearer—the soldier who rode alongside Joan, carrying the flag or banner that identified the army.**

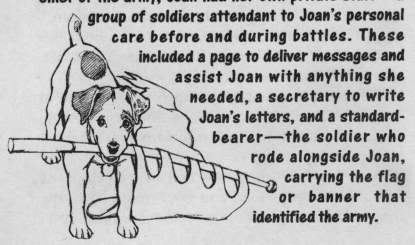

Joan turned to her friends with a warm and welcoming smile. "My dear friend Louis, would you step forward, please?"

Louis rose from his seat and came toward Joan. "Louis, it would be an honor for you to be my page and secretary," Joan announced. "You are my closest friend, and I need you by my side.

"Yes, Joan. I am, as always, your devoted friend and servant," Louis replied, and then his eyes became glossy, as if he were about to cry.

"And you, my brothers, Jean and Pierre," Joan said. "I need you to ride just behind me, with the two knights appointed by the Dauphin."

"Thank you, Joan," replied each of her brothers. "We are honored."

Then Joan called Paladin. Paladin hesitated before he walked toward her.

"I have been watching you ever since we left with the governor's men-at-arms," Joan began, "and you have grown to be both brave and strong."

That was all Paladin had to hear. He began to tremble and his eyes got very wide. He was afraid he had not been a good soldier. Paladin talked about brave deeds but did not always act bravely. But when he heard Joan of Arc tell him that he was brave, he *believed* it—and that was enough.

"I trust that you can and will be a great soldier," Joan went on.

Paladin's face brightened.

"Will you follow where I lead?" Joan asked.

"I will, Joan," answered Paladin with a strong voice. "And I will ride with great pride beside the wisest and bravest leader in France."

"Then you are my standard-bearer," Joan said. "Here is your banner."

Joan handed Paladin the banner. It was a beautiful white flag with red silk fringes, and it symbolized the authority of the King of France and God. Standard-bearer was the highest honor that could be given to any soldier. There were many generals, but there was only one standard-bearer.

Soon General La Hire joined Joan and the others. They all sat, laughing and talking like old friends. La Hire was entertaining and charming. Until then, Joan knew him only as a hero from her childhood—the great French general who fought for France's freedom. La Hire made Joan laugh, and it was obvious that the two were quickly becoming good friends.

At one point Joan heard a noise coming from the soldiers in the camp. Through the dense trees, she could see and hear soldiers shouting and swearing. They had been drinking and acting foolishly.

Joan became quiet and thoughtful, and then she turned to La Hire. "You are the master of this camp, and I need you to instruct the men to stop carousing, drinking, and swearing." Joan paused to think before

she went on. "The soldiers must be disciplined if they are to fight a war and win. Every man who is in my army must confess their sins to the priests. And they must be present at services each day," Joan added.

In Joan's day, priests traveled with armies to perform religious ceremonies and give advice. Today, priests in the military are called chaplains. They conduct services and give the soldiers comfort and advice during their difficult missions.

At first the general couldn't say a word. Then he responded in a strong voice. "Oh, sweet child," La Hire warned, "these men have lived rough lives, and they will live rougher lives as we go into battle. Attend services? Why, dear, I don't think they would even know what to do. They'll certainly refuse."

La Hire went on with his arguments, but Joan stuck to her point, and soon the general agreed. "I will try to do what I can. If you have given me such orders, I must obey.... And if any man in the camp refuses to go to confessions or services, I will knock his head off!"

Joan started to giggle. She found the general to be endearing, which he meant to be. "No, no," she said in a mild, lightly scolding voice. "I will not have you enforce my instructions with violence. Following my instructions must be voluntary."

"I will do as you ask," the general said with a sigh.

"I will announce the services in the morning, but I doubt there is a man in camp who is less likely to go than I."

"And you do not think you will attend?" Joan asked with mock surprise.

"I? Impossible!" snapped La Hire.

"Oh, no, it isn't. I need you to go to confessions and services each day along with all the others," Joan assured him.

"Oh, am I dreaming? Am I drunk—or is my hearing playing tricks on me? Why, I would rather go to—"

"Never mind that," Joan cut in. "In the morning, you will attend and it will become easy. Now don't look so downhearted. Soon you won't mind. You're going to be surprised when you see what happens.... Believe me. Have I been wrong before?"

"Well, I'll do it only for you, Joan," replied La Hire.

All the while, Louis and the others were listening to the debate between Joan and La Hire. They all agreed with the general that the soldiers would not want to follow these orders.

The next morning, only a few men attended the services. The last one to join the group was General La Hire, who fulfilled his duties grimly.

Yet within three days, the change in the camp was noticeable. The soldiers became clean and orderly, and all of them attended services. As the days passed, the men continued to be well-behaved. General La Hire was surprised at the men's devotion, and his admiration for Joan's wisdom grew.

Joan and La Hire became inseparable. They made an odd-looking pair as they rode side by side. He was so big, she so little; he was old and gray and she was young and beautiful; his face was dark and scarred, hers was fair and pink.

They rode together each night on the way to Orléans. They observed, inspected, and reformed any soldiers who behaved poorly. Wherever they appeared, the soldiers cheered and spoke with affection to show their great enthusiasm for their leaders.

Joan and her army were getting near to Orléans. Their first battle! I know Joan was able to accomplish a lot, but she hadn't ever actually fought like the great General La Hire had.

8
The Battle of Orléans

Joan and her army approached Orléans, which was surrounded by the English armies. To avoid a fight, she sent a letter that gave the English an option. They could leave French soil or stay and fight. Joan's proposal of peace was ignored. She confidently led her army into battle.

"Oh, there must be thousands of soldiers!" said a man in a horse-drawn cart along the road that led to Orléans.

"It's true. Joan of Arc has come to save France!" another man shouted with joy.

"Would you look at that? It's Joan of Arc and her army!" a farmer called out to his son.

"Here they come! They have finally come!" cried a woman carrying bundles under her arms.

All along the way to Orléans, admiring people followed Joan, trying to touch her as she passed. Many tried to kiss her shoes or touch her beautiful horse. For these people, Joan was the spirit of France made flesh.

The mighty and courageous army that Joan led

was a sight the French people had not seen in a long while. The men were a display of both strength and splendor. Long rows of armor-clad soldiers riding double file stretched into the fading distance. It was an inspiring sight to behold. All the soldiers sat tall in their saddles—particularly Paladin. Ever since Joan made him standard-bearer, he held his chin high and looked stronger as he rode on his horse.

When the army was just a few miles outside Orléans, they stopped in a small village to rest and replenish the food supply before the battle. Paladin went about the town gathering food provisions. He loved all the attention he received as he rode with his banner raised high, and felt great satisfaction as admiring people looked his way. He listened intently as he heard, "Look, it is the standard-bearer of Joan of Arc!" He entertained the townspeople with his exaggerated stories about riding with Joan of Arc. In Paladin's stories, *he* was always the great hero. When he stopped to speak to one woman, he learned important information that surprised him.

"I heard the English say they will attack the army led by the witch just as they're passing the fortress," whispered the young woman from behind her food stall. "They say it will be an easy win, since the French armies always run when they see English faces!"

Paladin immediately brought this news to Joan.

"You have done well, and you have my thanks,

Paladin," Joan said. "Thank you, dear friend. Your name and service shall receive official mention."

Paladin turned his head so that Joan could not see his tears. Louis noticed that Paladin was touched by Joan's confidence in him.

Joan turned to Louis. "Alert General La Hire. Tell him we must move out to Orléans now."

Soon the army was on its way. Joan took a position at the side of the road to watch the soldiers assemble. The soldiers filed by, some pulling carts with supplies. Joan noticed that a man was lying on top of one of the carts. His hands and ankles were tied together with ropes. Joan stopped the officer whose horse was pulling the cart.

"Why is this man tied up?" she asked.

"He is a prisoner," reported the soldier.

"And what is his crime?"

"He is a deserter."

"Tell me about him."

"He is a soldier, and he asked to leave the troops so he could go to his dying wife," began the officer. "We did not give him permission to leave, but he went anyway. Yesterday, he returned."

"He returned?" Joan asked, surprised that the man would return on his own. "Tell me then, how could this man be called a deserter? Bring him to me," she commanded.

The officer removed the ropes from the man's

feet. When the man stood, it was obvious that he was a strong and able soldier. He was almost seven feet tall, and his arms were muscular. He walked toward Joan with his head down.

"Hold out your hands, soldier," said Joan.

The man lifted his head when he heard Joan's soft, friendly voice. Then he held out his hands and Joan cut the ropes from his wrists.

Joan gasped when she saw that his wrists were cut and bleeding from the ropes. She called out, "Someone give me bandages for this man's wrists."

The man stared at Joan as she wrapped his wounds. He could hardly believe that he was receiving such kindness and care.

"There," said Joan as she finished with the bandages. "Now tell me why you left the army."

"My mother and children died in the famine last year. While I was away, I heard that my wife was dying," the man said softly. "I could not let her die alone. I begged for permission to go see her. The officers would not grant it. Forgive me, but I went anyway. My wife died in my arms. After I buried her, I returned to the army."

Joan looked into the man's face as he finished his story. Then she said, "No crime has been committed because you returned to your troop. You are pardoned. Now go and serve France."

The man was surprised and grateful, and his face

brightened as he called out in gratitude, "I will serve *you*!"

"You shall fight for France!" Joan responded.

"I will be *your* soldier!" he replied.

"You shall give all your heart to France!"

"I will give all my heart to *you*," the soldier continued, "all my soul, if I have one, and all my strength, which is great, for I was dead and am alive again. I had nothing to live for, but now I have! You are France for me. You are my France, and I will have no other!"

"Well, it shall be as you wish. What are you called?" asked Joan.

"My friends jokingly call me Dwarf because I am so tall," the man chuckled.

Joan laughed and said, "Would you like to be my man-at-arms?"

"If I may," Dwarf answered.

"Good. You will ride by my side."

"That I will," said Dwarf proudly. And Dwarf became a very faithful soldier—a protector—always attentive to Joan.

Joan joined General La Hire at the front of the army. Together, they led the soldiers toward Orléans. It was Joan's plan to march to Orléans and attack immediately. She gave this order to her captains.

A few of the officers thought Joan's plan to take Orléans was a mistake. "The battle should not begin so quickly, but should be drawn out over months," one captain offered. "By surrounding the English and cutting off their supply of food, we will eventually force them to surrender."

Joan did not agree and ordered the captain to follow the plan she had just given. But behind her back, the captains decided not to follow her orders. Instead, without Joan knowing, they led the army away from Orléans.

"In God's name," Joan complained when she realized the trick played on her. "We are on the wrong side of the river. You have disobeyed me. How can you not see that my plan is the only way? If you cut off the food to the English, you will be cutting off the food to the people in the city as well. God did not will me to this battle to starve innocent people while we starve the enemy."

Then General La Hire addressed the captains. "All you see is that Joan is young, but you do not see that she understands this war better than any of you. If you want my opinion, we have a lot to learn from her."

The captains were quiet.

"Precious time has been lost," Joan announced. She gave orders to attack Orléans.

Joan and her army reached the English fortresses outside of Orléans. Over seven months, they won battle after battle, taking forts and land from the English. Only

one important fortress still needed to be won to claim
the Battle of Orléans as a victory.

Joan and the army rode into Orléans for their
final battle. The men had been fighting for a long
time. They had fought bravely, but their hearts and
souls were weary. Joan did her best to rally her men for
this final attack.

She commanded the trumpets to sound the attack. Wielding her sword, she cried out, "If there are a dozen of you that are not cowards, it is enough! Follow me!" Joan rode off and her men followed, inspired as they looked toward their young leader.

What they found when they entered Orléans was very surprising: the English had fled the city. Joan and her men lowered their swords as they realized there would be no fighting just yet. Colorful banners hung along the streets and the people of Orléans enthusiastically welcomed Joan and her army. As the troops rode by, the crowds pressed forward. The townspeople had been hopeless, hungry, and afraid for so many years, and now that a French army had finally come, they could not restrain their desire to attack their enemy immediately.

"Attack the English invaders now."

"Storm the fortress!"

"The Maid of Orléans will save us!"

The voices from the crowd came one after the other, shouting their great hope for freedom. As the crowd continued to move toward the one remaining fortress, the growing excitement turned from celebration to conflict. The crowds pushed into the gates of the fortress. *Boom-boom!* The English fired cannonballs and arrows. *Boom-boom!*

"Charge! The English are ours!" Joan shouted as she rode ahead of the crowd and toward the enemy.

She continued to shout encouragement as the army fired their weapons and climbed the walls of the fortress. The French army and the citizens of Orléans pushed forward like a solid wave, killing all that came their way.

Suddenly an arrow struck Joan's shoulder. The sharp pain and the blood frightened her and she began to cry. The English shouted gladly from the fortress. They ran quickly to capture her. Fortunately, Dwarf stood over Joan and yelled, "For France!" as he swung his weapon at the attackers. He did the work of six men and prevented the English from taking Joan. Dwarf pulled the arrow from Joan's shoulder as she winced in pain. Forgetting her wound, Joan continued to fight.

The fighting continued for four days. When the battle was over, Louis, Paladin, and Joan's brothers went to look for her. They were worried—they had lost sight of her during the many days of battle.

"There she is," pointed Paladin with relief.

"What is she doing?" Louis asked, puzzled to see Joan sitting by herself among the dead. When they reached her, they found her with her face in her hands, crying.

"Oh, my dear friends and brothers," she said when she turned and saw them. "I have been thinking of the mothers of these men. It does not matter that they are my enemies. I mourn my friends and enemies alike."

Then she stood and smiled. "I am so glad to see all of you standing before me, unharmed." Tears flowed down her cheeks as she joined them. They hugged and walked together to their horses. Then Joan assembled the army and their English prisoners and returned to the center of the city. There, she gave the prisoners a choice: if they left Orléans immediately and never returned, she would free them. Otherwise they would be sent to prison.

When that was settled, Joan joined the celebration that had begun in the city. The French people of Orléans, who had been prisoners of the English in their own town, now filled the streets with laughter, dancing, and singing. Joan and the army moved through the thick crowd. There was not a heart that did not swell with love for her.

The crowd roared with enthusiasm. One triumphant and grateful voice after the other shouted with joy: "*Our* Maid! Victorious Maid of Orléans!" Many people reached out, trying to touch Joan. Yet all they needed was a glimpse of their liberator and heroine, the Maid of Orléans—merely to see the faithful and courageous Joan was to experience the mysterious feeling that she was sent by God.

9
Lady du Lis

Orléans had been won. There was only one more noble deed that God asked of Joan—to go to Rheims to crown the Dauphin the King of France. Then no one would doubt that France was on its way to freedom!

After Orléans, Joan and her army headed toward Tours to report to the Dauphin.

Word of the triumph at Orléans spread throughout the French countryside. Everywhere they rode, the people praised her. They came out to march or simply crowded around Joan as she passed by on her black horse. People even kneeled in the road and kissed her horse's hoofprints. Some of the most well-known and respected men of the Church wrote to the Dauphin, praising Joan by comparing her to the saints and heroes of the Bible.

The Dauphin reached Tours a day after Joan and her army had arrived.

"Charles the Victorious! France is saved!" shouted the townspeople as they welcomed their Dauphin.

Soon Charles sent one of his couriers for Joan. When she and Louis arrived, he was seated on a throne, dressed in one of his ridiculous costumes. He wore a crimson velvet cape, matching tight velvet pants, and a wide red felt cap from which his straight brown hair stuck out stiffly. At his side was his sword, and on his feet were pointy gold slippers.

When Joan and Louis reached the throne, they fell to their knees and bowed.

"Rise, Joan," the Dauphin said boldly.

Joan slowly raised her face to Charles. She looked pale and uncertain as she watched him. He removed his cap and swept his arm in a dramatic salute toward Joan—as if she were a queen. Then he stepped down from his throne, and walked toward her.

"You shall not kneel to me. You are the victorious General-in-Chief of the Armies of France," Charles said as he offered Joan his hand and raised her from her knees. "Come, child, you must not stand. You have lost blood for France and your wound is not yet healed." Then he led her to a seat and sat down next to her. Looking straight ahead, the Dauphin spoke.

"Now then, tell me what reward you would like for your courageous work. You have driven many Englishmen from our land. The victory at Orléans was a glorious battle and a noble deed."

Joan blushed. The thought that she would be paid for fighting for her country embarrassed her. "Your

Excellency," she said quietly, "I do not wish to be paid. What I do comes from my heart and my faith. I have been sent by God and only wish to fulfill my duties to Him."

Now the Dauphin was embarrassed. He realized that the best thing to do was to change the subject. They spoke of other matters but soon returned to the subject of payment.

"What reward would you like? You must want something!" the Dauphin persisted, baffled by her continued refusal.

"Oh, dear and gracious Dauphin," Joan finally said, "I have but one desire. Only one. If—"

"Do not be afraid to speak, my child," the Dauphin interrupted.

"My only wish is that you not delay another day," Joan continued. "My army is strong and valiant, and I am eager to finish my work. Please, march with me to Rheims Cathedral and receive your crown."

The Dauphin was quiet. Joan waited for a response, but he remained silent. Then he bent down to fidget with his pointy shoes.

"To Rheims? Oh, no, no. Impossible, my general," the Dauphin said in a rapid, nervous chatter. "My advisers would be totally against this. It is too dangerous to march through the heart of enemy territory...." He ended by looking nervously at his advisers, who were standing just a short distance away.

"Ah, I pray you do not throw away this perfect opportunity," Joan pleaded. "Everything is favorable—everything! The army is certainly a great enough force to protect and escort you to Rheims. The soldiers' spirits are high with the victory we have had over the English at Orléans. If we wait too long, we will lose this advantage. Now is the time, Your Excellency. Let us march!"

Joan rose and looked directly at the Dauphin. Louis noticed that her face displayed the same fierce passion as she had shown to Father Fronte years ago in Domrémy. Then she spoke in a low and serious voice. "If we wait, the English will gather the remaining men left in the countryside and strengthen their fighting force. What advantage will that have for us?"

"Why...none," the Dauphin responded uncertainly.

"Then what do you suggest?" Joan quickly replied.

"My judgment is to wait."

"Wait for what?" Joan was getting impatient but remained courteous. She again sat down next to the Dauphin. After a few moments of silence, she spoke gently and calmly. "Your Excellency," she pleaded, "there is so little time left."

It was clear from the Dauphin's face that Joan's words confused him, but he waited for Joan to continue.

Joan paused. "If I do not see you crowned King of France in a short time, I will never see it."

"Oh, you are wrong, my child," the Dauphin replied, slightly amused that she should be so dramatic. "You will live another fifty years or more. That little body is still strong, and you are a skilled soldier."

"No, Your Excellency. I will never see you crowned if you do not come with me to Rheims *now*," Joan said. "The time is short, and there is much to be done."

The Dauphin was moved by Joan's words. Louis noticed that the advisers whispered to each other when the Dauphin's face softened toward Joan. The Dauphin rose. He drew his sword and raised it above her head, bringing it down gently on Joan's shoulder.

"You are so simple and true and great.... So noble!" Charles exclaimed. "And for your noble mind and actions, it is only fitting that I make you a member of the French nobility!"

Joan was silent.

"I also hereby ennoble all of your family and all of your relatives, and their descendants, male and female," the Dauphin announced.

What an honor! To be ennobled means being made a member of the upper class of French society.

"Rise, now, Joan of Arc, and from here on, you will have the royal last name of *du Lis!*" the Dauphin continued. "All who address you will call you Lady du Lis. They will know from this name that you are royalty. And they will know that you are a soldier of the nobility when they see you carrying the royal shield. On this shield I will have engraved your royal name and France's emblem of nobility: lily flowers—the Fleurs-de-Lis."

Joan should have been proud, but when she left the Dauphin, she felt troubled. She was disturbed by all the attention. Having been born a simple peasant, she did not feel comfortable with her new name. She made sure that people continued to simply call her Joan of Arc.

10
Doubtful Dauphin

Joan and her army had been waiting for the Dauphin for weeks in a camp outside Tours. He had promised to march to Rheims, but, fearful that the roads were dangerous, he did not join her. Joan returned to the castle to convince the Dauphin to come now—and that her army would protect him.

"Noble Dauphin, I am begging you once again. Come quickly to Rheims and receive your crown," Joan pleaded. "What is it that prevents you from taking this last and glorious step to be crowned the one and only King of France?"

"I have been consulting with my advisers, Joan," the Dauphin replied. "And that takes time."

"Why must you continue to listen to your advisers? Don't you trust me to deliver you safely to Rheims?" she asked.

"I have told you. I cannot travel on the open roads toward Rheims if they are filled with the English. It is too dangerous," the Dauphin explained nervously.

Joan continued to plead, persuade, and reason with the Dauphin. When she could not convince him, she spoke with his advisers. They opposed her at every step.

"But the army is getting smaller and smaller," she cried. "Soldiers are leaving every night. I cannot stop them. They leave in the darkest hours of the night, when no one can see."

"It is true. I have heard. Soon there will no longer be an army," one of the advisers said with mock concern. "And what is an army without its soldiers? No army at all, of course!" he said, laughing.

"It seems impossible to march to Rheims now that our army is so small," another adviser added blandly. "It seems there is nothing we can do."

"Yes! There *is* something to do," Joan argued.

"What, my child, is that?" said the Dauphin.

"Raise a new army!"

"But that would take weeks to do, child," the Dauphin pointed out, half relieved.

"No, Your Excellency," Joan objected politely. "It will not take that long. Promise me this: when I return with my army, you will march with me to Rheims. I guarantee the army will be so large in number that as we march ahead of you, the roads will be cleared of all danger."

The Dauphin was listening closely now, and so were his advisers. "When you pass," Joan continued without a breath, "you will not see one English face...not one English cannon...not one English

crossbow. The land you walk upon will be yours. It will be French land again!"

Joan's speech was impressive, and the Dauphin agreed with the plan. So Joan returned to camp and made an announcement: "Join me and see Charles crowned King of France!"

By the end of a week, Joan had an army of thousands again. Many of the men who had left came back when they heard the news. With them came others who were enthusiastic and yearning to fight with the famous Joan of Arc.

Joan was in great spirits. She was here, there, and everywhere—all over the camp, by day and by night. It made her happy to hear the soldiers call out cheers as she passed. Seventeen-year-old Joan was a leader like they had never seen before.

A week later, the army marched out of the camp with the Dauphin in the rear. As the army made its way toward Rheims, many battles were fought to clear the enemy out of their path.

In one assault, Paladin was wounded. He was struck down from his horse and lay unconscious. He would have been trampled to death had Dwarf not been nearby. Dwarf quickly carried Paladin away from the fighting. Fortunately his wound was slight and Paladin rejoined the others. Soon he was swaggering around, bragging about his war wounds and his brush with death.

When three days had passed, Joan and her army reached Rheims and had reclaimed for France the land along the way.

"Oh, friends. Oh, dear friends," Joan called out to her troops. "Do you know? Do you comprehend? France is on the way to being free!"

La Hire shouted, "And it could never have happened without Joan of Arc!"

The men cheered wildly, and they—along with La Hire, Louis, Paladin, and Joan's brothers—shouted, "Live forever, Joan of Arc! Live forever!"

Joan smiled at La Hire and toward the vast army before her. Then she saluted with her sacred sword. Now there was nothing to stop Joan from completing her mission—and from seeing Charles crowned in Rheims Cathedral.

As they approached Rheims, they could see the great towers and sharp spires atop the cathedral. The Dauphin joined Joan at the head of the army. He rode toward Rheims with Joan at his side. Then came Paladin, carrying the banner high above his head. When they reached the town, crowds of people greeted them, cheering as the army came through the gates.

11

The Crowning Glory

Joan, the Dauphin, and the army entered Rheims to a magnificent display of patriotism. The town had been decorated in anticipation of their arrival. Colorful flags were raised, and music could be heard everywhere. Rows and rows of white lilies lined the streets toward the cathedral. Even the windows were filled with people, crying tears of happiness as they waved their handkerchiefs in the air. This was just the beginning. Tomorrow the Dauphin would be crowned the King of France!

The next day, the great Cathedral of Rheims filled with thousands of people wearing their holiday clothing. All the women and young girls were dressed in white jackets and red skirts to honor Joan, and on their necklaces were charms decorated with the emblem from Joan of Arc's royal shield.

Inside the cathedral, people were pressed against each other and every wall. The only open space was a wide aisle down the middle of the hall. Everyone anxiously awaited the beginning of the ceremony. Suddenly the doors of the cathedral opened and a hundred silver trumpets blew. The Archbishop of

Rheims and a group of churchmen entered and walked down the aisle. The Archbishop led them, wearing a grand costume and carrying a large cross in his hands.

Then a splendid sight was seen at the entranceway. Five stately men on their horses—the Archbishop's honor guard—rode down the aisle of the cathedral. They carried the holy oil that had been used to anoint all the Kings of France for the past nine hundred years. When they reached the altar, one of the horsemen handed the Archbishop the small bottle. Then they bowed their heads, turned their horses, and slowly pranced back up the aisle. At the doors, the horses turned toward the crowd and stood up on their hind legs. Then the honor guard spun around and galloped away. A deep hush fell on the crowd.

Then more music came from the trumpets. Framed in the archway of the west doors, Joan and the Dauphin appeared. They advanced slowly, side by side, down the aisle. Cheers and cries filled the cathedral, echoing from the high ceiling and walls.

Behind Joan and the King came Paladin, with France's noble banner held high. At his side was La Hire. They were followed by many other honorable men, including Joan's brothers and her faithful friend Louis.

When Joan and Charles came before the Archbishop, he recited many prayers. Then Charles took the sacred oath. "I, Charles the Seventh, the King

of France, will rule France with God's guidance. The French people's hopes will be my own." Then the King was anointed with the sacred oil.

After this, a group of attendants came forward with the crown of France upon a cushion. Kneeling, they offered it to King Charles—but he hesitated to take it. He put out his hand but stopped it in midair over the crown. Then he looked toward Joan.

"My gracious one, King of France," Joan whispered, "you are the only heir to the throne. Put the crown upon the only head that should rightfully wear it." She gave him an encouraging smile and the King grasped the crown, raised it, and proudly set it upon his head.

"France is saved!" roared the crowd.

"Long live the King!"

"Long live France!"

The organ blew out its thunderous music. The trumpets' silver song joined the choir and they all began to sing. Church bells rang and cannons boomed in the distance. France finally had its rightful King.

Before the King of France turned to walk down the aisle, Joan kneeled before him, bowing her head. Only Louis and a few of the others stood close enough to see that Joan's eyes were filled with tears as she raised her face toward King Charles.

● ● ● ● ● ●

Joan was finally seeing her dream come to life. The coronation completed her mission, and now she would be forever free of the war. She hoped to return home to her mother and father, and never leave them again.

12
A Dream Delayed

What a party! The town celebrated all day and into the night. Joan and King Charles paraded around the city for hours. When they finally headed toward the Archbishop's palace, where they would spend the night, the most wonderful thing happened....

"K neel!" yelled an officer riding ahead of Joan and the King. "Kneel! You dare to *stand* in the presence of royalty?" The officer was shouting at two peasants standing in front of an inn.

"Kneel, I said! Are you deaf? And look at you! No holiday clothing? Do you have nothing to celebrate today?" With that, the officer jumped from his horse and made his way to the peasants, whose faces were pale with fright as he approached. Just before the officer was about to strike one of the men, Joan turned her head in the direction of the noise.

"Stop!" she yelled as she leaped from her saddle. The officer moved aside as Joan approached.

"Father!" Joan called out warmly. She flung her arms around one of the two peasants. Then she turned to the other man, her uncle, hugging and welcoming him as well.

Nothing says "love" like a group hug . . . .

"Oh, my uncle! My father! How I miss my loving family! And Mother? Where is she?"

"Your mother is at home and was much too worried to make this long trip," her father said softly. "She worries about you day and night."

"Oh, poor Mother. I miss her, and it breaks my heart to hear this," Joan said in a sad voice. "I will be so good to her when I get home. I will do her work, and comfort her. My greatest wish is that she not suffer anymore."

Joan's brothers, who had remained on their horses up until then, jumped off excitedly. Louis and Paladin observed the loving family reunion from their own horses, as did King Charles.

After a few moments, the King called out in a commanding voice, "Joan, bring your family to me."

Joan led her father and uncle to the King. They were scared and hesitant. They removed their caps with shaking hands. Then awe filled their eyes as the King leaned from his horse and gave them his hand to kiss.

"Give God thanks that you are the father of this child, this noble soldier and heroine," said the King.

They bowed their heads, but the King's words made the two men even more nervous.

"These men are my guests!" the King announced to everyone as he waved his arm above his head. "And like nobility, they shall join us at the palace."

Joan's father tugged at her garments just as the King said this. "Joan," he whispered. "We want to stay at this inn tonight. We would not be comfortable at the palace."

Joan explained this to the King and he was understanding. He called to the innkeeper, who had been watching everything from the door of his inn.

"Give them your best service, and make a whole floor of your finest rooms available to them," the King demanded. Then he turned to Joan again.

"The city is giving a grand banquet for us. You and your family may stay at the inn tonight, but you must join the feast first."

Joan and her family, Paladin, and Louis followed the King and his staff to the banquet. There was much food and many speeches were given. King Charles and General La Hire spoke of Joan's bravery and wisdom, and praised her for the battle at Orléans. For Joan's father and uncle, it was a splendid spectacle, and tears ran down their cheeks as they listened to the honors that were paid to their darling Joan.

At one point King Charles put up his hand to command silence. Then, from somewhere in the hall, a tender and sweet voice began to sing a song that Joan knew well. It was one of the enchanting songs she and her friends had sung while playing around the fairy tree in Domrémy. As soon as this beautiful voice began to sing, Joan joined in; then her brothers, Louis, and Paladin did too. The song made Joan's heart ache. She remembered her childhood—her home, the rolling green pastures of Domrémy, and the fairy tree. The song ended and she put her face in her hands and cried.

When the banquet was over, Joan gathered her friends and family and returned to the inn for the night. They ordered some hot drinks from the innkeeper and went up to their private floor. When they settled into comfortable chairs, Joan looked at her family and friends affectionately and made an announcement.

"Now there will be no more ceremonies," she said. "We will be family and playmates again, as in earlier times."

Everyone felt happy and lighthearted. They spent the whole night talking, laughing, and telling stories. Joan's father asked many questions. He was very curious to know about the battles Joan fought and how Joan felt. It all seemed so amazing to him that his little Joan could do so much.

"I don't understand it," cried her father. "You are

so small and slender. Your armor must be very heavy. And now, in your pretty white silks and red velvets, you seem too dainty to be a general. It is very hard to imagine you in battles. Show me how you fought the enemy!"

"Of course, Father," Joan said happily. "Look. We march into battle like this." She held her hand on her sword and walked with authority. "And I carry my sword like this." She raised her arm as though ready to assault an enemy soldier. Then she playfully shouted commands and waved her sword in the air. "Here, you try," she said as she handed the hilt to her father.

Joan's father tried to imitate everything that Joan did. "No, no, Father. Not like that. Like this...."

They went on like that for hours. Joan uttered mock commands and her father excitedly obeyed like a playful child. They had a wonderful time, laughing and acting as they had when she was a child in Domrémy.

"But now I am done with these wars, Father," Joan suddenly announced in the midst of their games. "You will take me home with you, and I shall see..." Her voice trailed off and her face became serious. Doubts rose up from her heart, but she pushed the painful thoughts aside. "Oh, the day will come soon when—"

"Why, child," her father interrupted, "are you serious? Return home when you have done so much and received such high praise. There is still so much glory to be won."

"It is not difficult," said Joan gently. "God commanded me to the battle at Orléans and to crown the King at Rheims. My task is finished, and I am free."

"Would you leave the King and generals to be a peasant girl again?" asked her uncle.

"I am not fond of war and suffering," Joan replied. "It is not my nature to fight. I am happiest when I'm remembering our quiet times in Domrémy."

"Well"—her uncle reconsidered his last statement—"the villagers in Domrémy would love to see you again. They have heard so much about your bravery and are very proud of you. To honor you, they have named many of their children after you. There are many little girls running around Domrémy with the name Joan."

Joan was comforted as she thought about returning to her village, family, and friends—and the beautiful fairy tree. The great beech tree had never left her imagination, even when she was in battle. Joan was quiet and thoughtful, and there was a dreamy look on her face.

Suddenly that peace was broken.

"Joan of Arc's presence is requested immediately at the palace for a council of war," a King's messenger shouted across the room.

It took Joan a moment or two to recover from the

shock of what she was hearing. Slowly the sounds of military commands in the distance registered in Joan's ears, and the rumble of drums broke the stillness of the night. She knew that her guard was approaching. Deep disappointment clouded her face, but just for a moment.

"The King is my lord, and I am his servant," Joan uttered in a soft, low voice. Then she began gathering her belongings together.

It all happened so quickly. The homesick girl dreaming of returning to Domrémy became the great Joan of Arc, General-in-Chief of the French Army and ready for duty.

Joan had very little time to spend with her father and uncle. But she could not abandon her duties to King Charles. Everyone was saddened to see Joan leave. She and her father cried and hugged as they said their farewells. Then she left the inn and rode off on her horse toward the palace.

13

"O Gentle King"

Now that Charles had been crowned King of France, the battles ahead would be important. Winning back more French land from the English would make King Charles very powerful. The King's advisers wanted greater power too—over the King's decisions. They were afraid that the King would continue to follow Joan's advice.

Joan entered the hall where the council was meeting and looked around. The hall was cavernous. The ceilings were very high, and the thick stone walls were broken by long windows. Hanging from the walls were weapons, armor, and shields. Around a long, rectangular wooden table sat the King, General La Hire, and the King's advisers. Joan walked to the head of the table and looked toward the advisers. Her eyes were burning with purpose. When she had stared long enough, she began to speak stiffly.

"My business is with you. Isn't it?" she said to the advisers. "*You* have called this council of war...*not* the King." Joan was angry. Louis, who accompanied her in his official duties as secretary, noted that he had rarely seen Joan look so furious.

"A council of war!" she shouted. "The purpose of a council is to decide what is to be done. But who should make this decision? Wouldn't it be the one who is in charge? Am I not still commander of this army? Has someone else taken charge and not told me? "

Joan had a clever point. Louis was impressed that Joan had figured this out even before she got to the meeting, for she had come right in and immediately taken control of the situation. La Hire sat quietly in his seat. He knew Joan was right and that she had caught the King's advisers off guard. Watching them squirm as Joan stood over them amused La Hire. He clenched his teeth to smother his laughter.

Joan turned away from the advisers and looked toward the King and La Hire. "I will tell you what fight is before us! We march to Paris!" she declared. "If we win Paris, we will have won an even greater victory than at Orléans. That is where the English *and* the Duke of Burgundy are most powerful." **Most of the time Joan fought against the English, but there were also other enemies in France. The French Duke of Burgundy and his supporters fought against King Charles's family for many years. Because the English and the Duke of Burgundy both wanted to take land and power away from King Charles, they joined forces against Joan's army.**

"But—but, Your Excellency"—the King's chief adviser spoke up quickly, anxious to address the King before Joan said another word—"Would it be wise to fight Paris now? You may not know this, but we have been negotiating with the Duke of Burgundy, and he may soon pledge to return Paris to us. We would not have to fight and lose even one Frenchman."

Joan turned to the adviser with fire in her eyes. "You have taken military matters into your own hands? And you have had discussions with the enemy without consulting me?" exclaimed Joan. "You cannot be trusted!"

La Hire was so amused that he pounded his fist on the table as he tried to stifle another chuckle. The King looked amused too as his eyes widened and sparkled with pleasure. They were amazed at Joan's confidence.

"Sire, I ask your protection from such insults," pleaded the adviser as he stood up in shock.

The King waved him to his seat, saying, "Quiet. She had a right to be consulted before you approached the Duke—it concerned the war, and that is under her command."

The adviser seemed to shrink in height as every eye stared at him. Finally he sat down.

"O gentle King, let us march to Paris! The way is open. Paris calls us! Speak the word, O gentle King, and—"

"Does Your Excellency forget that the way to Paris is littered with English fortresses?" interrupted the chief adviser. "It will not be safe for you to travel—"

"*That*," Joan snapped, "is what you have told the King before. But the King already has proof that he has nothing to fear when he travels with my army.

"Come, my King," she continued. "We shall march to Paris, which will be the ultimate triumph for the newly crowned King of France!"

At that point La Hire rose and applauded. "By God, let us carry our lances to our great city of Paris and reclaim it," he said.

The King stood too. He drew his sword, took it by the blade, and walked over to Joan. Then he put the hilt of it into her hand, and said, "Here, take this, Joan. You are a wise general—a great soldier. Your advice has always been sound. Carry this to Paris!"

Only La Hire and Louis applauded. The advisers sat quietly in their chairs.

By the end of the week, the army was on the road again. Bands played and banners flew as they filed out of Rheims. Joan, her staff, and La Hire rode at the head; the King and his staff rode behind the army, protected by Joan and a buffer of thousands of soldiers who would clear a safe path to Paris. After only twenty miles, though, the King stopped at a small village to pray.

Joan and the army waited for the King to rejoin

them. She couldn't understand why the King was spending so much time in the church.

The King stopped only to pray, but his advisers had a plan. They again talked to the King about the dangerous roads and the enemy. As they hoped, this renewed the King's fears of continuing on with Joan and her army. What should have only caused a few hours' delay turned into days.

Meanwhile, Joan and the army were waiting for the King in their camp. After many days had passed, Joan dictated a letter to the King, pleading with him to join her:

Your Excellency, I beg you to come soon. The soldiers are beginning to get restless. We must keep our purpose clear and the soldiers inspired. I am sure that word of our delay has reached Paris. The enemy will have time to prepare for our attack. Follow me to Paris tomorrow, my King, or I fear we will have a rough fight.

Each day a new courier was sent with another note, and every time it came back with a promise that the King would join the army. But days went by and he did not come. Joan never thought the King would betray her, and couldn't understand why he had broken his word. She feared that her army would be weakened and discouraged when they found that the

King was not marching with them to Paris, but Joan decided to move on anyway.

Joan called Louis into her tent. "Louis, find General La Hire and tell him to prepare the troops to move out. I want the army on the road in the morning."

The next morning, Joan inspected the troops and spoke with all her captains and officials. Everything was in order. She mounted her horse, faced the vast army, and shouted, "Forward! To Paris, men!" Then she turned her horse and led the army out of the camp.

Four days later, when she and her men were at the walls surrounding Paris, she heard that the King had indeed come to Paris. She was pleased with the news, but what she had said in her note to the King was true. The English had made preparations to defend the city. After Joan discussed plans with La Hire, it was decided they might still win. Joan ordered her army to attack the next morning.

As Joan stood on the battlefield overlooking her troops, she was overwhelmed at the task before her. She gathered her courage. "For France! For freedom!" was Joan's call to her men as she rode before the gate. Her inspiring words led her men to the charge. They were determined to win Paris.

At the walls of the city, Joan commanded the army to storm the city gate. She was in the lead, with

Paladin by her side. When the army finally broke through, the assault began to rage. Clouds of smoke choked the soldiers and cannon fire flew over them like giant hail.

In the middle of the battle, when it seemed that Paris was about to be won, Joan was struck down by an arrow. Her injury was serious, and Paladin and Dwarf forced her off the battlefield. They would not allow her to return. As she was being carried off the battlefield, she repeated over and over, "I will take Paris or die!" When her soldiers heard that Joan had been injured, their morale weakened. They needed their leader, but she lay bleeding and was unable to rally her men to continue the battle.

Away from the fighting, Joan was sobbing. Not only the pain of her wound caused her tears—so did the realization that Paris had been lost.

14

A Prisoner Is Taken

Because Joan was wounded, the troops and the King lost courage. The men broke ranks and scattered, and the King returned to his castle. But with what remained of her army, Joan continued to fight the English and the Duke of Burgundy to reclaim more land for King Charles.

Joan and her army moved through the countryside, fighting one battle after the other. One day during a clash with the Duke of Burgundy and his army, Joan was wounded again.

"Victory is near!" she cried from the ground, waving her sword and trying to rally her troops, but her men ran off. This time, many of the soldiers believed that Joan had been killed. Discouraged, they couldn't go on without her.

Joan's personal guard, usually close by, was nowhere to be seen. Only Dwarf and Paladin were left. They would not give up, and fought valiantly to protect Joan from other assaults. Suddenly both Dwarf and Paladin were struck down. Joan was horrified as she lay on the ground, unable to help her dear friends. She tried to raise herself but could not. When Dwarf and Paladin waved their swords one last time and uttered their last words, Joan shrieked with grief. Their deaths were a tragedy. Joan lost two good friends and France lost two brave soldiers.

Still lying on the ground, Joan continued to swing her sword as enemy soldiers approached. But it became harder and harder for Joan to defend herself. With Dwarf and Paladin gone, she was alone. Suddenly from behind, she heard a roar of voices and metal armor clanging. Enemy soldiers were running toward her. Then she was seized and dragged from the ground by her cape. The Duke of Burgundy's army had taken her prisoner!

Word of Joan's capture quickly spread throughout the country. This was awful news for the people of France. They had believed that Joan was the only one who could drive the English out of France. People were dismayed, with one person after another repeating the same words:

"The Maid of Orléans has been taken!"

"Joan of Arc is a prisoner!"

"The Savior of France is gone!"

French people everywhere hung their heads and worried about their future. Joan of Arc had brought them hope, but now everything had changed. Joan of Arc would march no more.

• • • • • •

Joan's brothers, wounded and knowing of Joan's capture, returned to Domrémy. Louis remained in a town near the site of the battle for weeks, hoping to find out more about Joan. He heard that Joan had been taken to a prison in a town called Rouen (Roo-AN). Louis had many worried thoughts during this time. *Are Joan's wounds cared for? Is she still alive? Why has the King not paid a ransom to the Duke of Burgundy?* He decided to go to Rouen and do anything possible to help Joan.

Joan was desperately alone in her dark prison cell. Her wounds were taking a long time to heal and she was very weak. She wondered when King Charles would pay a ransom for her. Joan had committed no crime; she was a legitimate soldier and head of the armies of France by the King's appointment. By the laws of war, she could be freed if a ransom were paid. As the days passed and no one came for her, Joan's disappointment with the King grew.

Meanwhile, the news of Joan's capture and imprisonment had reached Paris. The English and the Burgundians were triumphant, and for days their bells and cannons rang through the city in celebration.

But the English and the Duke of Burgundy were not satisfied with simply imprisoning Joan. Joan was still alive. And they believed that as long as Joan was alive, she would continue to be an inspiration to the French people. This would make their task of ruling France impossible.

Louis continued to make his way toward Rouen to help Joan. When he was just outside Orléans, he heard more news about Joan from other travelers. Everyone in France wanted to know how Joan was doing, and news traveled fast. Louis was shocked by the stories he heard.

A bishop named Cauchon (Coh-SHON) had approached the Duke of Burgundy with a generous offer from the English. The English would pay a royal prince's ransom for the peasant from Domrémy. The Duke accepted this offer. Instead of Joan being ransomed by King Charles of France, she was sold to the English. The English could now put Joan on trial and attempt to prove that she was a criminal.

These stories made Louis feel hopeless. The more he heard, the more it seemed that Joan had no chance of being released from prison. He hurried to Rouen, determined to help her.

But when Louis got to Rouen, he was repeatedly turned away from the prison. Luckily, he met a priest named Manchon (Man-SHON) who had befriended Joan. Louis told him that he was also a friend of Joan of Arc's and he was trying to help her.

"Well, my boy," Manchon said, "I am the chief recorder at the trial of Joan of Arc."

"Father Manchon," Louis said, "do you think I could assist you in the courtroom? I too can read and write."

"I suppose it is possible," Manchon replied, "but you must not let anyone know you are a friend of Joan of Arc. That would cause serious problems for us all."

"No one will know. And I am sure Joan will not reveal who I am either," promised Louis. Then he asked Manchon more questions about Joan. He was extremely worried about her.

"Ever since Joan was sold to the English by Cauchon," Manchon told Louis, "the bishop has been busy gathering judges who will help him destroy Joan's good reputation. And he has appointed himself to lead the trial."

"But what are the charges that Cauchon has brought against Joan?" asked Louis.

"Ah, they are very serious accusations," Manchon said slowly and sadly. "She is accused of being a witch and of committing heresy." **To commit heresy means that a person has not followed Church law. During Joan's lifetime, heresy was considered a crime punishable by death!**

Louis was dumbfounded. What he had heard made no sense to him. Joan had always been faithful and religious. And as each day passed, Manchon came to him with more dreadful news about Joan.

"Louis, I have heard terrible stories about Joan," he said. "She is being kept in a dark and damp dungeon, surrounded by brutal guards.... She sleeps on a cold, damp stone floor and does not get much food. She is even chained to a bed by her hands and feet...*and neck*!"

Louis sat in silence with his head in his hands for a long time, thinking of poor Joan. His heart ached and tears poured down his cheeks. To imagine Joan in a prison cell and chained to a bed was more than he could bear.

"The trial is to begin tomorrow," Louis said sadly. "Then I will be able to see how my dear, beloved friend is doing."

15

The Great Trial

The next day Louis and Manchon went to the court. As they walked to their seats, Louis looked around at the dreadful spectacle. The room was filled with rows and rows of people who had simply come to watch. And at the front of the court were at least fifty church officials dressed in heavy red robes. Manchon pointed out Bishop Cauchon to Louis. He was dressed in the grandest robes of all. Louis's heart sank. *What chance does this simple country girl have against these men?*

"Bring forth the accused!" shouted Cauchon.

Louis jumped when that thunderous voice made the announcement. Then Joan entered the chamber. *Clink-clank, clink-clank.* She was marched into the court in heavy chains! Louis could see Joan was weary and worn from her captivity. What a small figure she seemed!

Joan's head was bowed and she moved slowly as she walked through the courtroom. She wore loose men's clothes. The shirt was black and had a wide collar that lay in folds upon her shoulders. The sleeves were short, and chains were wrapped around her wrists. On her legs she wore black pants that stretched down to her ankles.

As Joan walked to the bench, she passed through a ray of sunshine that came in from a nearby window. She stopped. A brief smile crossed her face and for a moment she basked in the sunlight as it warmed her cheeks. There was only darkness and cold in the dungeon. It had been a long time since she had felt the warmth of the sun's rays.

Louis could see that Joan was very pale—as white as snow. She looked thinner and more worried than he had ever seen her. But he could still see the gentleness that was always in her eyes.

Joan seated herself on the bench. Then she gathered her chains into her lap, clasped her small hands together, and laid them on top of the chains. Her sadness seemed to pass away at that point. She straightened her back and sat in a noble posture very much like when she rode on her horse at the head of the army.

Joan's mind was alert. She knew she was in a lot of danger. She had learned that the court would be made up of Cauchon and other judges who were in favor of the English. She had protested, saying that in fairness there should be an equal number of French judges, but Cauchon refused to make any changes.

The trial began when Cauchon summarized the case against Joan. Louis began to record everything he heard.

"Joan of Arc," bellowed Cauchon when he

finished his summary, "kneel before this court and pledge that you will answer with exact truthfulness all the questions asked."

"No," responded Joan in a soft yet defiant voice. "I do not know what you are going to ask me. And I will not pledge to answer questions that God does not want me to answer."

A low murmur came from panel of judges. It was obvious that Joan had angered the court. She remained calm, but Cauchon became excited.

"We require that you swear with your hand upon the Bible that you will answer all the questions truthfully!" shouted Cauchon. And then his hand came crashing down on the table in front of him.

"I will gladly speak of things concerning my father, my mother, my faith, and what I have done during my years in France," Joan answered in a steady, calm voice. "But I am forbidden to talk of the revelations I have received from God. My voices instruct me to speak of them only to the King."

There was more murmuring from the court and Bishop Cauchon had another angry outburst, demanding that Joan reveal everything the voices told her. In the midst of his ravings, Joan spoke again.

"You should know that I will *never* reveal these things to you—even if you threaten to cut my head off!"

This made half of the judges stand up in shock, and they raised their fists and yelled at Joan. They kept this up for several minutes. Joan, meanwhile, sat calm and untroubled by the noise. Three hours went by while the judges debated the situation and Cauchon repeatedly demanded that Joan take the oath.

"I will only take an oath that I propose," Joan responded at one point.

The angry judges calmed down slightly when they heard this. Then there was quiet while they paused to consider her idea. Cauchon broke the silence.

"You may take the oath that you wish," he announced in a cold, annoyed voice.

Joan slowly went to her knees. The chains rattled as she knelt down on the cold floor. She laid her hand on the Bible and recited an oath of her own making. When she was done, Cauchon began to ask her questions:

"What is your name?

"Where were you born?

"What is your age?"

He went on and on with questions about her family, her education, and other questions that were not important. After many hours of this, Cauchon started to tire and prepared to end the day's session. But first he delivered one more threat to Joan.

"If you try to escape from prison, you will be instantly convicted of all your crimes with no further trial!"

"You may speak all you want," Joan shouted. "If I can escape, I will."

The next day, Joan was again brought to the court in heavy chains; and again she sat on the bench and pulled her chains into her lap. Then Bishop Cauchon opened the session.

"You are required to take the oath to answer all the questions asked!" growled the bishop.

"I made my oath yesterday. That is the only oath I will take."

The bishop kept insisting, and his temper rose. Joan shook her head over and over again. At last the bishop gave up and the questioning began.

"When did you first hear voices?"

"I was thirteen when I first heard a voice coming from God."

"From which direction did it come?"

"From the right...from the direction of our church."

"What did the voice sound like?"

"It was a noble voice. And I knew it was sent to me from God."

"What did this voice say?"

"It told me to live rightly and to do service for the Church. Then it told me that I must save France."

"Did the voice seek you often?"

"Yes. Twice or three times a week it would say, 'Leave your village and go to aid France.'"

"What else did it say?"

"That I should go to Orléans to win an important battle."

"Who advised you to wear a man's clothing? Did your voices advise you this?"

"I believe my voices gave me good advice. I've done well to do whatever was commanded of me."

"Do you still hear the voices?"

"They come to me every day."

"You have said that you were sent by God. Is that not true?"

"I came from God. I am sent by God. I have nothing more to say."

On still another day, far into the trial, Cauchon went on again with questions about Joan's voices.

"Do your voices forbid you to tell the truth?"

"If I choose not to speak of something, it does not mean that I do not speak the truth," Joan responded. "I have always said that I was not permitted to tell you everything.

"I will say again as I have said before, I have answered questions of this sort already. If you bring the records from the commission that questioned me long ago in Chinon, you will see that I have already been sanctioned by the Church. It was declared that I had followed my faith and had not sinned."

Joan ended her speech with one demand: "Let us examine those books!"

But there was no answer to Joan's request. **Cauchon knew that those books could not be presented because the decision that Joan's mission was from God and that the Church permitted Joan to wear men's clothing was recorded in them.** Instead Cauchon changed the subject of his questions, as he had done so many times before when Joan had caught him in his own trap.

Soon Cauchon closed another long, weary session in court. Every device that Cauchon could find to trap Joan into admitting wrongdoing and disloyalty to the Church had not succeeded. But nothing would stop

Cauchon. He would continue to take advantage of her young age and her innocence. And by attacking Joan, who was cold, hungry, and tired, he hoped that she would eventually surrender to his demands.

Day after day, Joan was brought to the court. She was given very little food and water, and was not provided with additional clothing for warmth during the wintry months of the trial. Joan would sit for many hours on the backless bench with her chains in her lap while Cauchon assaulted her with questions. Over the five months of the trial, Cauchon asked her questions about her childhood, the fairy tree, the fairies, the games they played, and many, many more. Sometimes, when memories of those days—at home in Domrémy with her family—were stirred, Joan cried a little, but she would quickly stop and regain her noble posture.

During one of the last days of the trial, Cauchon gave a long speech instead of questioning Joan. Toward the end, he presented Joan with a choice.

"Among the answers that you have given, Joan, there have been lies. You have endangered our great religion and you are ignorant of the Bible. But if you desire to repent, you must first confess all of your wrongdoing."

"I have nothing more to say," said Joan.

With this refusal, Cauchon grew angry. "If you do not submit to the Church, you will be pronounced a heretic and burned at the stake!"

"I will not say anything different than I have already said," countered Joan. "And if I die, I beg you to have me buried in holy ground."

Cauchon and the court of judges were clearly disturbed by such defiance. But many who were in the courtroom were not. Some people gasped and cried out when they realized that Joan might die.

The next day, Cauchon announced that Joan was guilty of the crimes against the Church. But he told her that she could save her life if she did not commit any of the sins again.

"If you do not wear your men's clothing anymore, perhaps your life could be saved." Cauchon also promised Joan that she would be transferred to a more comfortable prison and she would have female attendants.

Joan was exhausted. The questions, the lack of food and warmth, and the continuous abuse made her feel weak and defeated. She thought for a moment and then answered, "If you will give me the dress of a woman, I will wear it. Then take me to that prison and let me be."

Joan was escorted back to prison. She was dazed and weak. She had not eaten in days. She was given a woman's dress and locked up in the same cell she had been in for months. And there she remained. Cauchon did not fulfill his promise. From that moment on, Cauchon made Joan's life in the dungeon even more difficult.

16
Saint Joan

Cauchon did not want to send Joan to her death without proof of her sins. He wanted to present to the people of France proof that Joan was a heretic and unworthy of their love and respect.

One morning, Joan went to put on her clothes, but the dress was gone. The only clothing in her cell was the men's clothing that she had worn before. During the night one of the guards, upon instruction from Cauchon, had stolen the dress. The only thing Joan could do was to put on the forbidden garments. This was all according to Cauchon's plan to trap her.

Seeing Joan in men's clothes, Cauchon now had the proof that he wanted. Joan was to be charged with being a relapsed heretic. **Joan had already been accused of being a heretic. A relapsed heretic meant that she had committed the same sin again. By calling Joan a relapsed heretic, Cauchon could claim that Joan again disobeyed the rules of the Church that she had agreed to follow. Her crime was punishable by death.**

The next day Manchon and Louis were called to the prison by Cauchon. They were to record what was said in Joan's cell. When Louis saw the cell, he began to feel sick. Joan was chained to the bed and wearing filthy clothing. She looked frail. The stone walls were damp and rats and mice scattered as everyone tried to fit into the tiny space. Joan felt comfort having Louis close by, although she could not show it. She displayed no emotions and hardly moved. When everyone was gathered, Cauchon spoke. "I condemn Joan of Arc to die for her crimes against the Church."

Louis could not control his grief. Tears poured down his face. Joan, sitting on the edge of her bed, dropped her head and began to tremble.

"And how will I die?" she said in a weak, shaky voice.

"By fire!" shouted Cauchon.

"Oh, I knew it," cried Joan. "I knew it!" She sprang wildly to her feet and began to sob. "Oh, you are so cruel to treat me this way! I had the promise of the Church—your promise—that I would be spared if I wore the dress of a woman."

"And you did not keep your promise, Joan," Cauchon said coldly. "You have returned to your sins."

"But I was tricked. Someone took my clothes! If you had put me in the other prison and given me the proper guards as you had promised, this would not have happened.... This is your doing."

Cauchon winced, then he turned and ordered everyone to leave Joan's cell. But Louis could not bear to go. He fell on his knees at Joan's feet and sobbed. Joan bent down and whispered in his ear, "Do not reveal our friendship, good heart. God bless you always." Louis felt the quick clasp of Joan's hand. His hand was the last hand Joan's would touch in her life. Joan stood, crying and wiping her eyes as Louis walked out of sight.

Later that night, Manchon brought Louis news. "I have just come from the prison," he said, "and I have a message from Joan. She would like you to write a letter to her mother."

"What does she want me to say in this letter?" Louis asked.

"This is what she said: *Tell my adoring, loving family, and all my loving village friends, that I cannot be rescued. I have seen the vision of the fairy tree.* Then she said that her parents would understand."

Louis knew Joan's letter was a message to her family and friends that they should banish any hopes of her return. The fairy tree had become a symbol of God's will, and now God had willed that she should die. It broke his heart, but Louis wrote the letter.

The next day, Joan was brought out of the prison in the wooden cart used to carry prisoners to their execution. She was brought to the old market square,

which was filled with hundreds of people. Louis was there, and watched with horror as the cart brought her to the center of the square. Everyone in the crowd was quiet as Joan was led up to a wooden platform and stake. Then her crimes were announced:

"Joan of Arc is guilty of crimes against the Church. She is sentenced to burn at the stake."

Louis broke down in tears. He felt as though he would never stop crying.

Once Joan was tied to the post, she turned to a soldier standing near to her and asked for a cross. He didn't have one but bent down and picked up two sticks, which he tied together and handed to Joan. She kissed the cross and held it to her chest. The priests recited a prayer and asked one more time if Joan would admit her guilt.

"I am to die," she said in an even, quiet tone. These were her last spoken words. She raised her eyes to the heavens and God's love filled her. She was no longer afraid of dying.

And so Joan died. People that witnessed her death cried and kneeled in prayer. The French were not convinced of Joan's crimes. Throughout the trial, Joan had remained true to her God, King, and country. Regardless of the trickery, treachery, and deprivation, she was courageous. All the people knew this and they continued to love and admire her.

Twenty-three years after the trial, King Charles appointed a commission to examine the facts of the trial and Joan's life. With the backing of the Pope, Joan was declared a noble patriot of the French people and a good and faithful servant of God. They could destroy her body, but not the memory of Joan.

The greatness of Joan's deeds has been carried to many people through the centuries. In 1920, Joan was given the highest honor bestowed by the Catholic Church—she was declared a saint.

You know, I've read
about a lot of heroes, but Joan of Arc
has got to be one of my favorites. Not only
was she brave, noble, and honorable, but she also
led the entire nation of France to freedom—and
she was just seventeen years old! It just goes to
prove that it doesn't matter who you are or how old
you are. If you believe in doing something with
all your heart, you can do it.
Till next time—see ya!